"I say, Holmes, you never told me you had a brother Sigerson."

"I never told you I had a brother Mycroft, either, till the occasion arose—the occasion has arisen."

- A vital document has been stolen from Lord Redcliff's safe.

- The fate of England depends upon its return.

- A voluptuous beauty with sexual hang-ups holds the key to the mystery.

- There is only one way to the key—and only one man who can take it. . . .

THE ADVENTURES OF SHERLOCK HOLMES' SMARTER BROTHER

An astounding, brain-boggling mystery of blackmail, intrigue and . . . *spine-chilling sex???*

THE ADVENTURES OF
SHERLOCK HOLMES'
SMARTER BROTHER

A novel by
GILBERT PEARLMAN

From the screenplay by
GENE WILDER

BALLANTINE BOOKS • NEW YORK

SBN 345-24671-3-175

First Printing: December, 1975

Cover art by Richard Ross

Printed in the United States of America

BALLANTINE BOOKS
A Division of Random House, Inc.
201 East 50th Street, New York, N.Y. 10022
Simultaneously published by
Ballantine Books of Canada, Ltd., Toronto, Canada

Chapter I

ONE OF THE MOST extraordinary episodes in the annals of crimes and their punishments began on a cool, crisp London night in the year 1891.

Most of the city's good citizens were fast asleep, including one of the most eminent among them, Lord Redcliff. His Lordship, Britain's globally esteemed Foreign Secretary, slept soundly in his large, comfortable bedroom, which was lit by the glow of a warm fire.

While he snored very softly, briefly relieved of weighty matters, a shocking bit of business was taking place elsewhere in the room. A slender, gloved hand deftly turned the combination lock of the safe on the bedroom wall. Soon, the night's silence was broken by a slight snap as the safe opened.

The snap produced the sudden appearance of Lord Redcliff's enormous police dog at the bathroom door. He stopped his imposing frame in the doorway, his strong white teeth bared and gleaming. As he was trained to do, he let out a low, vicious growl.

The great beast walked cautiously toward the safe while the intruder's two gloved hands unfolded a piece of tissue paper, revealing a key, and delicately removed a red dispatch box from inside the safe.

The box was opened with the key. A rolled document was taken carefully from the box. The box, with equal care and lightness of touch, was replaced inside the safe. The safe was closed and the combination lock was spun.

The black-and-brown dog, swallowing his growl,

whimpered. The safecracker, clutching the document with one hand, pet the dog with the other. Amazingly, the dangerous animal sniffed agreeably and licked the hand that pet him.

On a subsequent crisp night, which followed closely on the heels of the night of the theft, a related adventure occurred.

A large man entered a dark, empty room. He slowly shut the door, then crept toward a window, which looked onto London's widely known and highly regarded Baker Street. He was wearing an open overcoat and carried a strange kind of cane in his hand.

The cane, with a twist here and a click there, was transformed into a powerful air gun. With the cruel, bolt-blue weapon assembled, the man noiselessly raised the window about a foot. He crouched down and rested the barrel of his rifle on the ledge of the open window. The airless room was filled with the sound of his gasping, asthmatic breathing (a breathing long noted in the files of Scotland Yard, identifying the gunman as Colonel von Stulberg). He cuddled the rifle butt into his shoulder and took aim.

The rifle was aimed across Baker Street. The deadly accurate pinpoint of the aim was directed at a second-storey window, where the silhouettes of two male forms familiar to all Englishmen could be seen. One form was tall, the other stout; both were framed by a fire's glow.

The colonel moved his rifle to the left, following his gun sight to a dark window in the corridor of 221-B Baker Street, just to the left of the flat where he had spotted his two human targets.

Suddenly a lantern flared at the corridor window, its to-and-fro swaying obviously a signal to the waiting marksman.

The lantern illuminated the face of its holder. It was a face with a twisted lip, belonging to another man known throughout London's underworld—this one by the name of Bruner. His lantern message sent, Bruner turned from the window and crept along the corridor until he reached a door. It was one of the most respected doors of the Victorian Age, for on it printed letters announced:

S. HOLMES
Consulting Detective

Bruner set his lantern down and knelt, putting his deepest-set eye to the keyhole of the door.

What he saw through the keyhole was the famous Mr. Sherlock Holmes and his constant companion, Dr. John H. Watson. They were sitting now, appropriately and comfortably, in their puffy chairs in the sitting room of their flat.

Dr. Watson was clipping an article from a newspaper while drinking a cup of tea. Holmes was sending up huge puffs of smoke from his enormous pipe while busy at some small, indiscernible chore with his hands.

What the twisted-lipped spy could not see was a large stack of rectangular cards resting on Sherlock Holmes' lap. And that the celebrated detective had just finished marking the top card with a black crayon. He flipped the card over for Watson—and Watson alone—to see. It read:

> UGLY, 6-ft. 3-in.
> MURDERER AT KEYHOLE

Watson looked up casually from his news clipping, as he took another sip of tea. It was then he saw the card, and it was then also that he spilled his tea.

"Holy Jesus Christ—!" he muttered, over the splosh of hot amber liquid.

Holmes flipped another card:

```
┌─────────────────────────────────────┐
│                                      │
│   ACT NORMALLY                       │
│                                      │
└─────────────────────────────────────┘
```

"—but it's cold outside," Watson managed to continue, drying himself with a hanky. "Not that it isn't a nice night, mind you. Bit chilly perhaps, yes, but— bloody *damn* nice all the same."

Holmes flipped still another card:

```
┌─────────────────────────────────────┐
│                                      │
│   ASK ME ABOUT                       │
│   BESSIE BELLWOOD                    │
│                                      │
└─────────────────────────────────────┘
```

"What?" the doctor faltered, then blustered into recovery. "Oh! I say, Holmes, what did you think about Bessie Bellwood?"

"Who the devil is Bessie Bellwood?" Sherlock asked for the benefit of Bruner, who remained glued to the keyhole.

"Who the devil is—?" Watson broke the thread again, then retied it with, "Well, she's, you remember— young music-hall singer, flaming red hair, came round to see you this afternoon. Said she was being black-mailed, or some such thing."

"Oh, yes!" Holmes volleyed. "Colored chalk on her right thumb and forefinger. Why? What did *you* think of her?"

"The girl contradicted herself every other sentence," Watson replied. "Some sort of a crackpot, if you ask me. Too trifling to bother with."

"My sentiments exactly."

Holmes smiled, resuming his card flipping with a touch of whimsy:

TSK! TSK!

"Hmm?" Watson pondered.
Holmes flipped another card:

MOST IMPORTANT CASE
OF MY CAREER!

"What?!" the startled Watson responded. It was,
after all, a rather stupendous statement his friend had
made—the "most important case"—his friend whose
career had been built by solving so many important
cases.

"So, Watson," Holmes resumed aloud. "What do
you make of all this stolen document business?"

Bruner continued his watch as Watson exclaimed,
"Well! Must be pretty important indeed if the Queen
contacts you."

"So it would seem," Holmes agreed. "Her Majesty
suspects the French. She also believes that unless the
Redcliff document is back in our hands by Thursday
night, this country will be involved in a devastating
war."

"Holmes!" his colleague protested.

"Oh, well." Sherlock shrugged, conceding, "Perhaps
she exaggerates. We have two and a half days. You
know my thinking, Watson. How would you proceed?"

"Seven forty-five to Paris."

"Bravo! I don't suppose you've figured out some
ingenious plan for us to leave the country without
tipping off every murderer and petty thief in England
as soon as we step foot on the train?"

"Well, that's the sticky part, isn't it?" Watson asked,
pouring some tea into his cup.

"Is it?" Holmes answered the question with a question. "That article you're clipping states that S. Holmes is busy in his own country, meddling in other people's business."

Bruner pressed his undesirable flesh against the clean corridor door, fascinated.

Watson countered Holmes with, "But how the devil can you leave England tonight and still have the name S. Holmes appearing in all the London papers?"

"Quite simple!" the brilliant sleuth explained. "While Sherlock is gone, he shall pass on one or two of his *less* urgent assignments to his younger brother, Sigerson."

Watson jumped up, spilling tea on his pants, as the clock on their mantel gonged loudly.

"Oh! Seven o'clock already," Holmes said, flashing at Watson another card, which read:

> EASY!

"We should be starting for the station," Sherlock continued, rising.

Watson forced himself to be calm, blotting his wet, bothersomely hot crotch with a hanky, and demanded, "Holmes! You never told me you had a brother Sigerson!"

Holmes emptied his drooping pipe.

"I never told you I had a brother Mycroft, until the occasion arose."

"Well, now that you mention it, no. But—"

"The occasion to mention Sigerson has arisen!" Holmes concluded.

Bruner raced back to his former position at the dark corridor window. He waved his lit lantern frantically back and forth.

The gun-loving colonel across the street caught the signal, much to his dislike. He didn't approve of the change in plan. Nevertheless, he immediately withdrew his air gun from the window ledge of the empty room and began disassembling it.

"Next time, Holmes, ya lucky bastard," von Stulberg grunted, packing the rifle back into its cane form. All the while, he glared across Baker Street with fearsome disdain.

Chapter II

A FEW MOMENTS LATER, Sherlock dragged out an old photograph of three boys and set it atop the stack of cards he had earlier used as a communication system with Watson. He identified the subjects in the photo while he and the doctor packed.

On the left of the crinkled picture's trio stood a pudgy, seventeen-year-old. He was Mycroft, the oldest of Mr. and Mrs. Holmes' three boys. In the middle stood a ten-year-old Sherlock, thin as a rail and (even then) wearing a deerstalker cap. And finally, on the right, was a five-year-old who was staring at Sherlock with what certainly seemed to be hatred in his eyes. The cherub with the lethal stare was Sigerson.

"But who is the fellow now?" Watson asked, as he and his dear friend secured the straps on their luggage. "Where is he? What's he been doing all these years?"

"Sigerson, as I said, is my younger brother," Holmes repeated, not as curtly as he might have, considering how he abhorred repeating himself. "He lives not far from here. At number Nine Balfour Place. And he has spent most of his thirty-five years getting hopelessly twisted in my shadow."

"Poor devil! Extremely jealous, is he?" Watson commented, putting on his coat and taking another glance at the expression on young Sigerson's face in the faded photo.

"Something of that sort," hummed Holmes, putting on his coat.

"Love and hate, eh?"

"I should say—hate and dislike."

"Holmes!" Watson admonished him.

"Oh, I'm sure that underneath it all he really does have some affection for me," Sherlock admitted. It was a rare sentimental admission for the solidly intellectual detective—and, in truth, he didn't know whether or not he believed it himself.

On Baker Street, the two renowned Londoners secured themselves a hansom cab. They moved off through a dense fog, headed for Victoria Station.

The ugly, murderous, and eavesdropping Bruner waited at the station. He leaned against a platform pole and lit a cigarette. His eyes were in the constant motion of search.

Sherlock Holmes and Dr. Watson walked along the platform, up to Bruner and past him. At the very moment of passing the cutthroat, Holmes turned to his companion with a suggestion.

"Croissant and hot chocolate when we arrive in Paris. How does that sound to you, Watson?"

"I shan't make the mistake of using the bidet this time, Holmes. Nearly broke my ass," Watson observed as the two men entered a train car.

On the platform, some people passed in front of Bruner, forcing him to strain to keep Holmes and Watson in sight. Then his vision was blurred for a while by passengers rapidly passing back and forth on the train.

After a moment, the view cleared again. And Bruner smiled contentedly as his eyes distinctly caught his prey through the train window. He saw Holmes in his deerstalker cap, smoking his enormous legendary pipe. At his side was Watson, in his top hat, about to read the paper.

The eagle-eyed Bruner could not see *inside* the car of the train, of course. If he had had the advantage of an inside view, he would have seen a very tall, thin lady with a long nose, dressed in Holmes' cape-backed overcoat and deerstalker. She was smoking Holmes' classic pipe and clutching a five-pound note.

And next to her, at the window, he would have seen a very stout lady. She was dressed in Watson's overcoat and top hat. Reading his newspaper, she also clutched a five-pound note.

Bruner missed, too, their single, delighted verbal exchange.

"Strange fellows!" said the tall, thin lady.

"Very generous, I must say," said the stout lady.

While Bruner basked in murky satisfaction, the real Holmes and Watson stepped off the train just as it started to move on its journey to Paris. Holmes was dressed in the clothes of the tall, thin lady, complete with high-heeled shoes and hat. And Dr. Watson was dressed in the stout lady's outfit.

They walked along the station platform, toward the ever-alert Bruner.

"I still don't understand why we're going through all this bother," Watson pointed out as Holmes was taking a cigarette from his borrowed, satin-grained purse. "If the case is so bloody important, why aren't you handling it yourself?"

"Because it all revolves around a woman, Watson. And a woman, I fear, who must fall very much in love before she's capable of trusting anyone."

"Ahh."

When they reached the spot where Bruner stood, still watching the train with the intensity of a hawk, Holmes held up his cigarette to him.

"Could I trouble you for a light?" the detective asked, daring to use his own, natural voice.

The beastly Bruner reluctantly lit the cigarette, but not for a second did he take his eyes off the departing train.

"Thank you so much," Holmes offered pleasantly. He and Watson walked around Bruner and then came together again, continuing down the long stretch of station platform.

Watson seized the opportunity, his first since racing to the train, to plunge back into the night's main topic of discussion.

"I suppose you've seen Sigerson about all of this."

"Seeing my brother in person is much too upsetting to him," said Holmes.

"Written?"

"I would never entrust the mails with a matter of such delicacy."

"Well, then, I assume you've selected a messenger who will present him with all of the essential information."

"Even as we speak, Watson," Holmes assured his skirted partner, as they came upon a man in a bowler hat who was carrying an umbrella and wore a sandwich board advertising

RED HERRINGS

"Even as we speak," Sherlock repeated, swiftly passing a five-pound note to the promoter of red herrings. "One Orville Stanley Sacker, by name. Sergeant in the records bureau—Scotland Yard."

"Bright fellow, is he, this Sacker?" Watson asked.

"Not in the least," Holmes stated, gazing back for another look at the sandwich man's bowler hat.

"But how can you trust him?"

"Ah! Trust is his one indelible virtue. For delivering messages *exactly* as they were given to him, he has no peer in England."

"Don't say."

"Yes!" Holmes did say, emphatically. "He's the only man I've ever met who has a photographic sense of hearing."

"My word!" the doctor mused. "Never heard of such a thing."

Chapter III

ORVILLE STANLEY SACKER, the messenger supreme with a photographic sense of hearing, left Victoria Station, dumped his sandwich-board disguise, and quickly set out for the other side of town.

Clamping his trusty bowler hat on his head, he fought wind and fog until he reached 9 Balfour Place. He climbed a long flight of stairs. When he made it to the top and into a hallway, he spotted his goal—a shingle above one of the doors, marking the residence of:

S. HOLMES
Consulting Detective

Orville dutifully knocked.

The door was opened by Sigerson Holmes. Mesh covered his features, for he just happened to be wearing a fencing mask over his head. Without saying a word, the younger Holmes took Orville's hand. He studied the man's fingernails, hat brim, and the sole of his right shoe.

"Have a nice time in Constantinople, did you?" Sigerson asked smugly.

"You have just made a very wild guess," stated Orville.

"I never guess," Sigerson rapidly and firmly replied. "Guessing rots the brain. I observe twenty-three to twenty-eight infinitesimal facts within a thirty-second period. That's why I don't think, but *know,* that you've been in Constantinople—within the past three months. Am I right?"

"Not quite," Orville answered.

"Call me a liar for a month or two—say the past *six* months."

"Closer," Orville teased.

"The past year!" Sigerson snapped.

"No."

"*Two* years!"

"No."

"When?"

"Never."

Sigerson Holmes let a significant moment of silence pass by. Then he took off his mask and, his eyes unmeshed, looked hard at Orville Sacker.

"Do you assume," he began coldly, "that I have nothing better to do with my time than to stand in a corridor and play word games?"

"I'm sorry," the caller apologized, glancing at the other man's boldly angular face. "Are you Mr. S., for Sigerson, Holmes?"

"Perhaps."

"You do have a brother whose first name is Sherlock?"

"I do not."

"Hmm," said the man in the bowler, thoughtfully. "You do have a brother?"

"Yes," Sigerson finally admitted.

"Might I inquire as to his first name?"

"*Sheer-luck!*"

"I see," replied the caller, pleasantly. "Well, your brother Sheerluck has sent me with a very urgent request—*and* a five pound note." He held up the five pound note he had been given at the station. "Are you at all interested?"

"You can tell my brother," Sigerson spitted out between his gritted teeth, "to take his five-pound note and—"

"And may I say," Orville interrupted before receiving the full instructions as to the disposal of the five-pound note, "that I've been an admirer of yours for many years. Especially your handling of the Case of the Three Testicles."

"You've studied the Three Testicles?"

"Orville Stanley Sacker," the man formally introduced himself. "Sergeant. Records bureau. Scotland Yard. A pleasure, Mr. Holmes."

"Come in, Orville," said Sigerson, changing his tone and taking the fiver. "I was just making some tea."

Orville followed his gracious host into the flat.

Sigerson's home, Sacker could see when once inside, wasn't really a flat. It was one room, one long room. There was a screen at one end, separating the living area from an improvised bedroom.

It was a poor man's dwelling. However, the music-hall posters that adorned the walls gave the place a warm bath of color.

Giving the place a bit of a weird feeling, on the other hand, was a huge bicycle wheel with a seat on top of it. It stood next to a strange mechanical contraption, which, by some stretch of the imagination, resembled a man in a fencing position.

"Just hop on that bicycle seat, will you, Orville?" Sigerson asked his guest. "I won't be a minute."

Young Holmes then went over to a small table next to the contraption. He checked out the table-top contents: a fencing foil, a fencing glove, a towel, a water pitcher, and a glass. He put on the glove and picked up the foil.

Meanwhile, Orville turned his attention to taking a closer look at what he concluded to be the Fencing Machine. The thing had bent legs; a large red heart, isolated in its chest by springs; and a right "arm" that held a foil. On what might be called its neck sat a stuffed head with a silly smile.

Sigerson, beginning to limber up in preparation for a bout, shout-sang away: "Ay la-la-la-la-la-LA! Ay LA! La-la-la-la-ayyy LA!"

After his guest looked first at him and then at the stuffed head of the machine, Sigerson commanded,

"Come on! Come on! On the bicycle seat! We haven't got all night!"

Orville obliged. He climbed onto the bicycle seat.

"Start pumping!"

Orville, still in his coat and bowler hat, dutifully did as he was told and started to pedal and pump. The pedals went round and round, but the bicycle didn't move. Rather, through the motion of the pedals, a wind-up propeller attached to the back of the Fencing Machine began to whirl away, clockwise.

"All right now, keep a steady pace," Sigerson directed. Whereupon he saluted the machine and began to fight it.

The machine, contrary to Orville's expectations (as it would be to any reasonable man's expectations), fenced magnificently. Parry, thrust, thrust, parry—a veritable mechanical master.

Sigerson stopped for a moment, addressing Orville. "Do you think you could pump a little faster?"

Orville pumped a little faster. Sigerson and the machine fenced a little faster.

"Don't be timid," Sigerson shouted. "I said go *faster!*"

Orville, however, was getting tired and stopped for a rest. Breathlessly, he began to inquire, "I wonder if I could—"

"PEDAL! PEDAL!" Sigerson commanded. "For God's sake, man, don't just stop in the middle like that."

"Sorry." And the exhausted man began pedaling again.

"What do you think this is," Sigerson bit at him, "—a *toy shop?*"

The youngest of the Holmes boys fenced furiously, as did his mechanical opponent. Thrust, stab, parry, and pierce. Human superiority finally triumphed when Sigerson succeeded in hitting the machine's heart. The stuffed head tilted forward abruptly, accompanied by a grunt from somewhere within the nuts-and-bolts innards.

Orville, very much relieved, stopped his pumping.

"Sucker!" Sigerson shouted at the machine, taking off his fencing mask.

"Quite a fellow," Orville volunteered.

Sigerson gulped a glass of water and then informed his guest, "He's the seventeenth best fencer in Europe." He wiped his face with a towel as Orville climbed down from the bicycle seat.

"Now then," said Sigerson, walking to a tea table in the teatime section of his room and pouring a cup. "What's this urgent request?"

Orville joined him at the tea table.

"Due to ill health," he began his message, "your brother has decided to take a short vacation in the country. Oh, not very long, two or three days at the most, but he would very much appreciate—"

"Sit down, won't you?" Sigerson asked his guest.

"Oh. Thank you."

"Pray continue." He handed Orville a cup of tea.

"Thanks!" said Orville, taking the tea, after which he resumed. "Due to ill health, your brother has decided to take a short vacation in the country. Oh, not very long, two or three days at the most, but he would—"

"Milk?"

"Just a drop, thank you very much."

"You were saying?" Sigerson pushed on, pouring a few drops of milk into Orville's cup.

"Due to ill health, your brother has decided to take a short vacation in the country. Oh, not very long, two or three days at the most, but he would very much appreciate it if you would be kind enough to—"

"Sugar?"

"Oh! Thanks very much." And the amazing man with the photographic sense of hearing took a spoonful of sugar.

"Yes, go on."

"Due to ill health, your brother has decided to take a short vacation in the country. Oh, not very long, two or three days at the most, but he would very much appreciate it if you would be kind enough to handle one of his *most* urgent cases during the time of his absence. All fees going to you, of course."

Orville sucked in a deep portion of oxygen.

"I see," Sigerson deduced. "His way of saying he's *stuck!* Anything else?"

"He has taken the liberty of sending round Miss Bessie Bellwood, of Chislehurst, to whom he hopes you can be of some service."

"Bessie Bellwood?"

"Yes."

"Are you sure the name is *Bessie* Bellwood?"

"Positive," Orville confirmed. "Bessie."

"I see." The youthful consulting detective strolled a short stroll. "I'm busy just now, but this case might present one or two points of interest. At any rate, we shall know presently. For, unless I'm very much mistaken, the young lady's dainty hand is just about to knock upon my door."

There was, precisely at that moment, a knock on the door. Orville was impressed. He stared at Sigerson in amazement, but Sigerson waved off his knowledge as a simple matter of logic.

"Come in!" Sigerson implored. *"Miss Bessie Bellwood of Chislehurst."*

Chapter IV

THE DOOR DID OPEN.

And someone did enter.

But it was not a dainty lady.

It was a lumbering giant, Hunkston, the building's porter.

"A young lady is downstairs to see you, sir," Hunkston managed, awkwardly trying to hold his bulk still. "Shall I show her up?"

"Show her up! Show her up" an impatient and angry Sigerson ordered. He continued to shout orders as Hunkston left the room. "And quit tippy-toeing around out there! Walk like a *man,* for God's sake."

"Perhaps I had better—" Orville suggested.

"No, no, sit down!" his host insisted. "I find your presence comforting, somehow."

There was a new knock on the door. Sigerson opened the door quickly.

There stood before him a beautiful face. It belonged to a curious figure of a woman whose inherent elegance didn't at all match the odd clothes and tatty boa she was wearing.

"How do you do," the woman crooned. "My name is Bessie Bellwood."

"LIAR!" Sigerson roared at her.

"Wow!" she exuded. "This is quite a first meeting. Ooooh, have you ever got blue eyes. I'm not saying you're right—but if you were, why *would* you be right?"

"Because you aren't Bessic Bellwood," the adamant, blue-eyed detective replied."

"Do you know Bessie Bellwood?" the woman asked.

"Never met her in my life," he admitted.

The lovely lady paused. She reflected. Then, she offered her hand again. "How do you do? My name is Bessie Bellwood."

"LIAR!" Sigerson had another good shout.

"Whew!" she whistled. "You don't fool around, do you? How do you know that I'm not Bessie Bellwood?"

Sigerson began singing:

> "There's no harm
> in taking a kiss.
> It's never missed."

The woman immediately jumped into the song, picking up the lyric:

> "If I'd known
> love is like this,
> Should I have kissed?"

The blond-haired detective eyed her intently, then continued in song:

> "Love's a game
> if you are clever,
> Play your cards and go."

The woman, too, continued to sing:

> "Love with me
> will last forever,
> That is all I know—
> 't you don't love as I do,
> You can't love as I do.
> Sometimes, I'm—"

Sigerson finally interrupted her. "All right, all right!" He returned to silent reflection, while the woman, still standing in the doorway, glanced at Orville and smiled.

"Hello," she said.

Orville half rose off his chair and nodded a hello. Holmes suddenly burst into song again:

"Piggy, piggy, piggy, piggy,
Piggy, piggy, pooh,
Cried the farmer's daughter Phyllis."

The woman appeared to be stumped. She began humming to herself and valiantly, although unsuccessfully, tried to fake a song she obviously didn't know:

"Piggy, piggy . . . piggy pig . . ."

She gave up, regretfully admitting, "I don't think I know that one."

"Pity!" Sigerson retorted harshly, triumphant in deduction. "The next time you decide to impersonate a music-hall singer who's been dead for twelve and a half years, I suggest you learn her full repertoire. Now, won't you come in, Miss *Liar*."

"Thank you. What a charming flat you have," she commented quickly, entering the room and walking toward Orville.

Sigerson closed the door and followed her with an introduction. "This is my good friend, Orville Slacker."

"Sacker!" his good friend corrected him.

"Sacker! Sorry." Sigerson stood corrected. "Orville, may I present Miss *Liar*."

"How do you do? Very pleased to meet you, I'm sure," said Orville in the nicest of manners.

"*Merci bien*," Miss Liar replied.

"Won't you sit down?" her host offered.

"No thanks, I can't stay." She sat down. "Your brother Sherlock certainly is a character."

"My brother is a very insecure man. Now then, precisely what is it that you want of me?"

"Well, I have this friend."

"LIAR!" Sigerson bellowed again.

She sighed. "*I* am being blackmailed."

There was a gleam in Sigerson's eye as he sensed he finally was on the path to truth.

"May I offer you some tea?" he asked, softening his attack and holding the tea tray before her.

"No, thank you," she said, taking a cup of tea.

"Exactly who and what are you?" the detective demanded.

"My name is Jenny Hill and I'm a serio."

"A what?"

"A serio. I'm simultaneously funny and sad."

"How interesting. Do you know who's blackmailing you?"

"Eduardo Gambetti."

"Gambetti? Hummm. Milk and sugar?"

"No thanks," she said, taking milk and sugar.

"Eduardo Gambetti," Sigerson returned to the subject at hand. "Ever heard of him, Orville?"

Orville held his head erect, tapped his temple, and began conducting a dialogue with himself: " 'What, not Gambetti again?' . . . 'Fraid so, sir.' . . . 'Fat little fart? Fashions himself an opera singer?' . . . 'Yes, sir.' . . . 'Pour us some tea, would you, Sacker?' . . . 'Yes, sir.' . . . 'How the hell does he do it, Grierson?' . . . 'Pays the highest prices for spicy letters. Everything in the market goes to—oh, thank you, Sacker—everything in the market goes to Gambetti.' . . . 'The Swine!' . . . 'Swine he may be, sir, but he certainly is cleverest of all the blackmailers.' "

His remembered conversation repeated and completed, Orville quietly returned to sipping his tea. Jenny and Sigerson stood transfixed, staring at him.

Jenny broke the silence, although still stunned at Sacker's recitation. "I'm not sure I— What just happened?"

"Never mind. I'll explain to you later," Sigerson assured her, shaking his head in admiration of Orville's capacity for total recall. "The swine wants money from you in return for what?"

"I'm being married in two and a half days. Gambetti promised not to show my fiancé a foolish letter that I wrote to a silly young man I met in the country."

"What was in the letter?"

"Oh, it was nothing," she protested. "It was just a frivolous, innocent little—"

"*What* was in the letter, Miss Hill?"

"Wouldn't you call me Jenny?"

"What was in the letter, Miss Hill?"

"By the way, do you mind if I call you Sigi? Sigerson seems so formal."

"What was in the letter, Miss Hill?"

"I said I wanted to touch his winkle!" Jenny confessed at last.

Sigi let a pregnant pause go by before he muttered, "I see."

"Good-bye," said Jenny, rising with the same abruptness with which she had confessed.

"His *what?*" asked Orville.

"Nothing!" Sigi said to his friend, promising, "I'll explain it to you later."

Jenny turned to the second gentleman. "So nice to have met you, Mr. Cracker."

"Sacker," Orville maintained.

"You're leaving?" Sigi asked.

"Yes," she answered. "I have to be at the theater by ten. I hope you won't think too unkindly of me, but everything I've told you just now has been a lie. I was trying out some new material for my act."

"I see! Just a few laughs, eh?" Sherlock's brother smirked.

"Yes, that's the idea," Jenny prattled on. "I was walking along and then I suddenly saw your winkle on the door—I mean I suddenly saw your *shingle* on the door and thought to myself, Why not? If I'm lucky I might just get a fresh, unsuspecting audience."

"Well, you were very lucky indeed, then, weren't you?" Sigi suggested.

"Yes!" she spluttered, trying hard to hold back tears as she made her way to the door. "Today is really my— I'm just—what can I say? You've been so very kind. A little too gullible perhaps. I'm sorry if I took advantage of you. Don't feel badly. I'm sure God would much prefer us to be a little too vulnerable, rather than—"

"Jenny!" Sigi snapped.

The lady stopped.

Sigerson Holmes gave her a short, compassionate glance and then, again without notice, burst into song:

> "Have you seen the latest
>   dance that's come along?
> Jenny, go and put your Sunday
>   hat and jacket on."

The lady maintained her silence. The detective stepped up to her, continuing his song, softly and tenderly:

> "There's going to be some jolliky,
>   Come with me, happy be.
> Fill your heart with ecstasy.
>   Jenny—"

Jenny, a tear in the corner of her eye, joined him, half talking, half singing:

> "—it's the greatest thing
>   creation's ever known."

Sigi sang:

> "Take a little tip from me.
>   Hold tight—"

Jenny sang:

> "—I'm all right!"

Sigi and Jenny sang together:

> "When you do the . . .
>   H—O—P!"

Orville Sacker leaped from his contained shell and freely lent his voice to the occasion. As Jenny and Sigi began to lightly hop, the newly formed trio vocalized:

> "Come on and
>   Hop, hop, come and do the
>   Kangaroo Hop, hop.

That's the dance for me and you.
If you're over eighty
   You can waltz a little while.
But hoppin' about the parlor,
   Is the very latest style."

The two young rousers tugged at Orville until he joined them also in their dance. All three of them then were singing and Kangaroo Hopping wildly about the room. Their childlike vitality became an ode to the spirit of life.

Chapter V

THE HIGH-STEPPING TRIO in Sigi's place did not know that their impromptu performance was being studiously watched. But as they romped in innocence, the face of evil—Bruner—stood across Balfour Street, staring wide-eyed. Since he could hear no sound to co-ordinate with the action, his view was that of three crazy people, hopping silently like berserk kangaroos.

Bruner scurried to his employer, who was none other than the infamous Professor Moriarty, renowned as Mr. Sherlock Holmes' arch rival.

In Moriarty's lab, Bruner told the master criminal of the unusual scene he had just witnessed, while the latter held and fondled a pet rat in his hands. Next to the professor was his assistant, Finney, who, like Bruner, sported a twisted lip.

"Hoppin' like kangaroos—heh, heh, heh," Moriarty laughed. "That's wonderful funny. I love that."

"It's almost time, Professor Moriarty," Finney volunteered, fidgeting with his watch.

"I know, Finney, I know," the professor answered. "But this is fascinatin'. I'm dyin' to hear what comes next. Go on, Bruner."

"Well, sir—"

Bruner was stopped cold by a high-pitched, involuntary yelping from Moriarty.

"YUH! YUH!"

The shrill, eerie yelps were immediately followed by the same Moriarty insisting, "Pay no mind, Bruner. Go on with your report."

It was like being asked to pay no heed to a bat in

your hair. Bruner's nerves were shattered, but his mission was his report and he was devoted to any mission assigned to him.

"Well, sir, after a few moments of this hopping—"

"YUH! YUH!" The soprano yelps were heard again, backed up at once with "Go on Bruner, go on."

"—the three of them bounced out of the room."

"The three of them bounced out of the room! Heh, heh, heh!" The professor once more was highly amused, and his left eye began to twitch.

"It's really time, sir," Finney insisted.

The professor rose and handed the grey, jagged-toothed pet rat to his assistant. He put his arm warmly around Bruner's shoulders and started walking him past laboratory equipment and blackboards filled with mathematical equations toward an opposite side of the room.

"And you just left them there, Bruner? Ya didn't follow to see where the three of them might be goin'?" Moriarty inquired of his hired hand as his eyes launched themselves into a rolling motion.

Bruner had some difficulty in answering, watching as he was—in terror, in fact—the professor's eyeballs beginning to circle madly. At last, he forced himself to say "No, sir. I thought their behavior was so strange—"

"YUH! YUH!"

"—that I'd better come and tell you right away."

"I see."

"But I did hear them hail a four-wheeler carriage for the Tivoli Theatre on Jermyn Street."

"Heh-heh. Bounced out of the room. That's delicious," Moriarty mused. He stopped, stopping Bruner with him, at two large doors, one *red,* the other *blue*.

"Excuse me a moment," the professor said. He knocked on the *red* door.

"Yes?" asked a woman's voice from within.

"Is everything all right, Alicia dear?"

"Yes, Professor. Fine, thank you," the woman's alluring voice answered.

Moriarty knocked on the *blue* door.

Bruner's eyes bugged as the ferocious sound of a tiger growling was heard from behind the blue door. He gasped.

"I wonder if you'd do me a small favor, Bruner?" his employer asked sweetly.

"Anything, Professor. Anything at all."

"I wonder if you'd mind leavin' by one of these two doors. I've some official visitors comin' up the front stairs any minute now, and I'd rather they didn't see you leavin'. You don't mind, do you?"

"No, sir," Bruner slurped through his shivers. "I don't mind."

"Good lad," Moriarty congratulated him. "Either door, Bruner. The choice, of course, is yours."

Bruner studied both doors. Then, intelligently, albeit shakily, he chose to enter the *red* door, from where he had heard the unknown woman's siren voice call out. He closed the door behind him.

A few moments passed. Suddenly, from behind the red door, the incredibly resounding roar of a tiger was heard, as were the loud screams of Bruner screaming his way into hell.

Moriarty's eyes stopped twitching. His eyeballs ceased rolling. His face became calm. Refreshed, again a man whose emotions were in his control, he walked directly and with purpose to a dark corner of his laboratory.

It was a very dark corner, save a thin line of moonlight that shone in through a window. The beam from the moon ended as a tiny bright dot on a confessional, which Moriarty entered. He knelt in prayer.

A priest sat on the other side of the booth's grillwork panel, his white collar and thin red hair clearly visible. He listened.

"Forgive me, Father, for I have sinned," Moriarty confessed.

The priest nodded stiffly.

"It's the curse again, and I know you'll understand. Of course, it must be a great trial to your patience,

Father, but just think of the burden it's been to me."

The man of the cloth turned slightly, as if to hear the sinner better.

"The burden it's been to me ever since that day when my hereditary tendencies finally burst out into the open and I felt this irrepressible desire to do something rotten every twenty-four minutes. It's been very painful to me, Father. Comin' up with a real corker every twenty-four minutes is no simple job, I'm tellin' ya."

There was a sudden metallic noise, followed by a low buzz. The priest's face turned, revealing him to be a Moriarty invention: a rosy-faced mechanical figure sitting on a mechanical stool.

The professor reached into his pocket, producing a coin that he slid into a slot. His self-made priest nodded understandingly.

"As I was sayin'," the penitent picked up where he had left off. "If you could find it in your heart to forgive me, I'd be most grateful."

Music burst out, filling the booth, and a small, scented card slid down a shoot and through a slot to Moriarty's side of the grillwork.

The professor picked up the card and read it with relief, his lips forming its merciful word:

```
┌─────────────────────────────┐
│                             │
│   ABSOLVED                  │
│                             │
└─────────────────────────────┘
```

Chapter VI

ONTO THE STAGE OF the packed and bustling Tivoli
Theatre, Jermyn Street's thriving music hall, a covered
baby carriage was wheeled. A spotlight hit it.

A second spotlight hit three dandies, dressed in top
hats and tails, who were pushing the carriage. More
lights hit the cheap backdrop of nannies pushing baby
carriages in a park.

The three Fancy Dans pulled back the sliding cover
of the carriage and there was Jenny Hill, costumed as a
baby, sitting in it. She began the number:

> "I've got the sweetest
>   little dimple
>   in my cheek."

The men sang:

> "You love to show it."

And they lowered the front end of the baby carriage,
transforming it into a cute little stepladder.

> "I've got those
>   invitation eyes
>   that seem to speak."

The men sang:

> "You seem to know it."

The three top-hatters helped her down from the
carriage. Jenny stepped onto the stage with:

31

> "I've got the cutest
>   little walk,
> The cutest line of
>   baby talk,
> And deary,
> When it comes to kissing—"

Her abbreviated chorus line was right behind her:

> "There's nothing missing."

Sigi Holmes and Orville Sacker sat in the audience, in second-row seats. Both of them were enthralled with the lovely Jenny and her performance.

> "I've got that
>   linger-longer
> something in my smile."

The men sang:

> "And that's a blessing."

Jenny went on:

> "I've got that
>   'won't you kiss me?'
> wiggle in my style."

The men sang:

> "And we're not guessing."

The voices of Jenny and the men blended for the next lines of the number:

> "My feelings you must sense them,
> Words never could express them."

The dandies declared:

> "We're simply crazy over you."

And Jenny belted out the ending:

> "They're simply crazy over me."

The stage lights went out amidst enthusiastic applause. The lights returned long enough to allow Jenny and her chorus to take their bows. Sigi and Orville, as might be expected, were among the most emphatic in their applause.

Professor Moriarty's twisted-lipped assistant, Finney, sat in a box above the main orchestra section. He was apparently nervous, fidgeting and constantly looking at his watch.

What had Finney fidgeting was going on high above the Tivoli Theatre stage. There, a glove-handed catlike man—carrying a long, sharp knife—was making his way along the gridiron. He was crawling toward a three-dimensional cardboard replica of an 1891 motorcar. The huge, weighty prop was suspended by four ropes tied to a main cord.

What Finney might also have fidgeted about, *if* he had known of his presence, was a man—in disguise— slouching in his seat in the orchestra just in front of Sigerson Holmes. No one would have known who the mystery man was, so expert was his disguise, except perhaps his most intimate acquaintances: they might have noticed that he was holding an *enormous pipe* in his mouth.

Meanwhile, still high above the stage, the catlike man's knife accidentally made a tiny slit in a sandbag, one of those sandbags used for weight balancing in the world of the theater. He remained unaware of the accident as he immediately went about his business at hand. His business at hand being to slice the main cord that held up the prop motorcar.

Below, two veteran propmen carried a park bench onto the stage. A dapper man in tails, the adored and self-adoring Brewster Marsh, Tivoli's mainstay male performer, walked to the bench and sat down.

A thin stream of sand started to spill from the slit sandbag in the gridiron. And a small pile of sand started to build up on the stage floor. A grain of sand bounced off the stage, into the dark auditorium, and landed on Sigi's face. He casually brushed the sand away.

Handsome Brewster positioned himself, and his tails, comfortably on the bench on the stage. He whispered, "Ready?"

Jenny, now dressed in a new costume and having snuck onto the dark stage, positioned herself behind the bench. "Ready," she whispered back.

Her performing partner crossed his legs and lit a cigarette. The two veteran propmen rushed off, stage right, and into the wings.

The lights went on. The music went up. The song began.

Brewster led:

> "You should look
>   on love as an art,
>   and treat it so."

Jenny followed:

> "If you could
>   but see in my heart,
>   you'd never let go." -

Then Brewster:

> "Love's a book,
>   you turn the pages,
>   till the end you see."

Then Jenny:

> "Love will last
>   Throughout the ages,
>   there's no end for me."

In the orchestra, Sigi's face lit up with a great smile, for he was remembering Jenny and himself singing that song only a few hours earlier. Then, another grain of sand bounced off the stage, hitting Sigi in the eye. Again, he casually brushed off the sand.

Jenny continued:

> "But you don't love as I do,
> You can't love as I do.

Sometimes I'm sad,
But sometimes I'm glad."

High above the stage, Moriarty's gridiron man remained busy slicing the main cord that held the automobile prop. In his box, Moriarty's Finney clutched his cap nervously. In the wings, a man in a swimming suit, the next act, and the two old propmen approvingly watched Jenny Hill sing.

The pile of sand on the edge of the stage grew and grew. The Man in Disguise in the front row—the man with the *enormous pipe*—took a few grains of sand into his hand. He threw the grains over his left shoulder. Those same grains found their way into Sigi's ear. He brushed them off, annoyed, his attention still riveted on Jenny.

Jenny, during that particular turn in her performance, came downstage to sing directly to the audience. She now returned to her original position, behind Brewster and the park bench. At that point, the orchestra played a short musical bridge: "Toot, toot, ping-a toot, soo wup."

Also at that point, the disguised man with the pipe (who, yes, yes—as his intimate acquaintances might have known—was Sherlock Holmes) grabbed a handful of sand from the pile on the edge of the stage. He flipped the sand, with some force, over his left shoulder.

That handful of sand hit Sigi full smack in the face. Poor Sigi spit and coughed and wiped the sand from his eyes. Finally he looked up toward the gridiron. He rubbed a single grain of sand slowly between his fingers and submerged himself deep into thought.

Polished Brewster Marsh cleared his throat in preparation for the second verse of his song, and opened his mouth to sing.

The leading man, however, was not destined to sing his second verse that night. For Sigi took destiny by the throat, stood up straight in the orchestra, and let go in his best voice:

> "There's no harm
> in taking a kiss.
> It's never missed."

Jenny became cross-minded, and almost cross-eyed, in confusion. But, professional that she was, she didn't miss a beat. She picked up her cue and sang right to Sigi:

> "If I'd known
> love was like this,
> Should I have kissed?"

Orville surveyed his singing new friend with popped eyes. The people seated immediately behind Sigi were very confused, and a little angry. Brewster flipped; his senses drained out of him and he became lost onstage. He looked searchingly to the wings for help. None came.

Sigi was his own man and would brook no attempt to pull him off his course. Motioning Jenny forward, to the front of the stage, he continued his song (not without some secondary enjoyment over waxing lyrical to Miss Hill):

> "Love's a game
> if you are clever,
> Play your cards and go."

Jenny, mesmerized, started to walk toward Sigi. Brewster, engulfed in frustration, rose and followed her, trying to catch her eye, trying to break the spell.

Finally, sensing her leading man behind her, Jenny felt frightened. Her eyes searched from side to side. But the nightingale in her still sang:

> "Love with me
> will last forever,
> That is all I know—"

THUD! BRACK!

The prop motorcar fell from the gridiron and crashed onto the stage. It landed next to the park bench—the exact spot at which gorgeous Jenny would have been standing if Sigi had not urged her to the front of the stage.

Most of the audience jumped from its seat and screamed. Many did not notice that the man who once was high above the stage, the sharp-knife wielder, had plunged down with the cardboard motorcar. Having had no intention of plummeting with the car, he was stunned out of his wits.

Jenny turned in horror. She, too, screamed—the most desperate scream of all, as she understood what happened.

And the despicable cord cutter in the car quickly climbed out of the driver's seat and dartingly dashed off the stage, out of the theater. Not surprisingly, he was holding his crotch, for the prop car's gear-shift stick struck an excruiatingly painful target.

The orchestra, its musician members forever bent on being a calming influence, launched into a catchy, even jaunty, tune.

The two old propmen rushed onto the stage and gaped up at the grid, puzzled that one of their own brother craftsmen could have been so careless.

Sigi Holmes let the excited members of the audience dash back and forth in front of him. He slouched into his seat, arms folded, leagues deep in his own special brand of thought.

Chapter VII

THE HORSE pulling the four-wheeler carriage trotted diligently down the misty London street, clap-clap-clap-clapping as it went along its way.

Inside, Orville, Jenny, and Sigi rode. The latter was hunched up in a corner listening to the conversation between his two companions.

"Then since you first tried to get back your letter from Gambetti," Orville was saying, "he's raised his price three times?"

"Yes," Jenny answered.

"How much cash does he actually want from you now, Jenny?"

"None."

"I beg your pardon?" Orville was taken by surprise.

"Three days ago," explained the lady, "he suddenly told me I didn't have to pay him a penny."

Orville glanced at Sigi, who remained hunched in a corner and silent.

"I'm afraid something isn't making sense, luv," Orville suggested.

Jenny explained. "He said he'd give me back my letter if I would—" She hesitated, then went on. "If I would steal—" She sighed before finishing. "Steal a certain document from my father's wall safe."

Sacker tossed another glance at Sigi.

"What does your father do, Miss Hill?" Sigi inquired.

"He's the janitor at Browning's Bank in Clearwater Street."

"Browning's doesn't have a bank in Clearwater Street," Sherlock's smart brother reminded her.

"Poor Papa," she purred. "I wonder if he knows?"

"*What* does your father *do,* Miss Hill?" Sigi demanded again.

"How did you know so quickly that Browning's doesn't have a Clearwater branch?" Miss Hill asked Mr. Holmes.

"I *assumed* you were lying. What does your father do, Miss Hill?"

"One day you're going to *assume* a broken ass, *Mr. Holmes,*" the lady snapped, swinging her purse at Sigi.

Sigi ducked just in time, but Orville didn't and the purse smacked against his head. Orville slid, dazed, to the cab's floor. When he regained his focus and composure, he sat up again, but this time next to Sigi.

The persistent detective resumed his singular pursuit of information. "What does your father do, Miss Hill?"

"That was no accident, and you know it," she stated, ignoring his question, referring to the earlier incident at the Tivoli.

"I know nothing of the kind," Sigi insisted.

"If you hadn't made me move downstage, I would be dead now," Jenny said.

"Well," mused the detective, "as it happens, you are extraordinarily alive, your *lies* are of the same excellent quality, and I can't help you if you're going to become hysterical and act as if everyone around you is trying to hurt you."

Jenny started to defend herself. Instead, she froze—horrified.

She had looked away from Sigi for one brief moment, and she had seen a horrible face with a twisted lip staring at her from the window of a hansom cab on their right.

Jenny experienced a double freeze when she turned her head to the left. There, she saw another horrible face with a twisted lip staring at her from the window of another hansom cab.

"Scream! Scream! Scream!" the poor girl muttered tensely to herself.

"What are you saying?" Sigi asked.

Jenny pointed out the window. "I'm saying AAAA-AAAAAAAAAAAAAHHHHHHHHHHHHHHHHH!" she screamed.

Sigi and Orville quickly looked out of the windows. They had become the meat of a sinister sandwich as the three cabs, theirs in the middle, headed down a long dark stretch of street.

Orville looked to Sigi for direction. Sigi pondered, then poked his head through that strange and traditional hole, the cabby's latch, in the carriage roof.

With his head emerged into the night air, the detective looked from side to side. To his right, a mean, really *mean*-looking driver was smiling at him. To his left, another mean, undeniably *mean*-looking driver was smiling at him. And next to that driver, Moriarty's mean-looking Finney sat. His twisted lips, too, were curved into a smile. They were three nightmare smiles boding nothing but ill.

"How far are we from Piccadilly Circus?" Sigi asked his driver.

"Not far," the driver replied. "But there's a long dark stretch up ahead first. That's what the buggers to our right and left are waiting for."

"Pace yourself till we get there," Sigi instructed him. "Then try to outrace them. All right, Fred?"

"Right y'are, guv."

"If you run into trouble, give a loud knock on the roof and then pull up sharply."

"Yes, sir."

Sigi started back down into his cab.

"*Say!*" the cab driver yelled at him. "What made you call me Fred?"

"Fred is the eleventh most common male name in Britain," the brilliant thinker explained. "Your pronunciation of the *o* and *a* in 'long dark stretch' places your birth east of the River Thames—where Fred is the third most common name. And your *license,* Frederick Whittcomb, is nailed to the right-hand door of your cab."

The driver protested. "But my name is William. This is my nephew Fred's cab."

"Is that supposed to be clever?"

"What's that, guv?"

"Nothing!" Sigi retorted. "Just keep your eye on the road or you'll get us all killed."

"Yes, sir." William Whittcomb, uncle to Frederick Whittcomb, saluted his fare.

Sigi lowered himself back into the carriage, leaving the cabby's latch open. He took off his coat and his jacket and turned to Jenny.

"Anything really out of the ordinary you'd like to do before the race begins, Jenny."

"What did you have in mind?" she asked.

"Oh, I don't know," said Sigi. "Dance? Take a sponge bath? Tell the truth—something really crazy like that."

The pace quickened, and quickened again, as the three vehicles headed noisily down the street.

William the driver finally poked his head through the latch and into the carriage.

"No good, guv," he moaned. "I can't outrace 'em with our load. Their horses are too bloody fast."

"All right, get back," Sigi ordered. "I'm coming up." And he pulled his sword out of his sword-cane.

Precisely at that moment, for no apparent reason, Jenny Hill began to sing an old favorite of hers, "The Huntsman," at the peak-top of her voice:

> "Away, away, away, away, away,
>   away, away we go.
> I don't know where we go, but
>   still I know we go away."

"What *are* you doing?" Sigi asked incredulously.

"Whenever I'm petrified, I either cry or sing," she replied.

Holmes let her explanation go by without devoting

too much time to trying to understand it. He certainly didn't want her to cry.

Orville Stanley Sacker must have been petrified and required some sort of self-tested psychological support, too. His eyes became glassy, his breathing heavy. He began to recite: "London streets and places of interest—Abbey Road, Abbey Street, Abbeyfield Road, Aberdare Gardens . . ."

Sigi shook his head at both of them in disbelief, then struggled through the latch and climbed onto the roof of the cab. From inside the carriage, the litany of fear suppression went on and on.

Jenny sang: While Orville chanted:

I won't infer
that I never
hunted hares before.
Because at home,
when we had soup,
I've found them
by the score.
Away, away, away,
away, away, away,
away we go . . .

Abingdon Road,
Admiralty Arch,
Albert Memorial,
Apothecaries' Hall,
Army and Navy Club,
Ave Maria Lane,
Bank of England,
Bankruptcy Buildings,
Barnard's Inn,
Barnet Garden . . .

Chapter VIII

ZOOM! ZOOM!

The cabs zipped, slashing the air, eating up the street.

Sigi, on top of his surrounded cab, knelt at the right-hand edge of the roof. He held out his hand to his driver for support.

"Fred!" he called.

"Fred's in hospital, with swollen hemorrhoids," the driver answered.

"I mean *William*," Sigi corrected himself, and stored away the information.

"Yes, guv?"

"Give me your hand for support."

William extended his hand to Sigi, who leaned perilously far over to the right. He could see the street whiz by below him.

"Don't let me down, William."

"I bluddy well won't, guv."

Sigi leaned even farther to the right. The mean driver of the cab on the right began whipping Sigi mercilessly with his horsewhip. The brave detective took four stinging blows to the body. On the fifth blow, he deftly sliced the whip at the hilt with his sword, leaving the driver with only the handle.

The amazed driver gaped at what was left of the whip in his hand, and then urged his powerful horse on to a faster speed with his reins.

Sigi swiped the reins in half. The scrubby driver now found himself holding a whip handle in one hand and two short pieces of useless leather in the other.

"Anyone you care to be remembered to?" Sigi called out to his victim.

After a moment of reflection, the nasty driver replied, "Well, my wife maybe. An' the two little sons. Don't bother about my older boy. He's a mean bastard, no feelin' for anyone but himself."

Sigi swiped at the poor driver's hat and cut it cleanly in half. The driver felt his hair through his slit chapeau.

"Well," the desolate cabby confided, "time for me ta be gettin' home. Good night, guv!" At which point he jumped off the racing cab and disappeared into the London fog.

Sigi hailed his departure.

"Good-bye."

Inside the four-wheeler carriage, the man with the horrible face from the hansom on the left had just broken the window next to Jenny. He leaned through the shattered glass with a long, treacherously sharp knife in his hand.

Jenny, more terrified than ever, sang louder than ever.

"Away,
away,
AWAY . . ."

Orville hurriedly took off his shoe and plunged the sole of it onto the would-be murderer's knife. He doffed his bowler hat and began clubbing the cad over the head.

Crash! The man with the other horrible face, the ugly moose from the hansom on the right, broke the second window and leaned his head through its shattered glass. Orville hit one head with his stiff hat, then the other—back and forth, back and forth, like a mallet pounding against two anvils.

All through the hat-hitting anvil chorus, Jenny sustained her bellowing song and Orville continued his rundown of the great city's highlights:

"I don't know   "Bedford Avenue,
    where we go,   Bedfordbury,

> but still I know   Bedford Place,
> we go away . . ."   Bedford Road . . ."

The roof-riding Sigi had another instruction for William. "All right—*switch!*"

William switched the reins into his right hand, offering the swashbuckling hero of the night his left hand. Sigi leaned far toward the cab on the left.

The driver on the left, in full command of his brutal reflexes, whipped Sigi soundly. His cohort, Finney, urged him on, keeping his own sleazy eyes glued on the point of Sigi's sword. When Holmes was about to wield his weapon, Finney rose, revealing that he, too, was armed with a whip. Crack! He knocked Sigi's sword completely out of his hand.

Finney's driver interrupted his thrashing of Sigi long enough to smile with bloody anticipation.

"Evenin', Mister Holmes," Finney leered. "Won't you come and join us?"

"Well . . ." Sigi stalled, then prepared to jump onto their cab.

The barrel-biceps driver gave Sigi two stout blows with his whip. Before the third blow could land, Holmes caught the whip with his arm. He yanked the second nasty driver toward him, kicked his heel into the man's square chin, and sent the wretch sailing off the cab onto the damp, cold street.

Sigi, adjusting the whip into the proper position for intelligent fighting, addressed himself to Finney's previous invitation. "Join you? All right—but just for a few minutes."

Turning to his own driver, he commanded, *"Let go of my hand, Fred!"*

"Fred's still in hospital," the cabbie reminded him.

"William! *William!* You can let go now."

"Good luck, guv!"

Sigi leapt. He successfully landed on Finney's cab, but in the process took a fierce blow across the shoulder from Finney's whip. Finney, in turn, accepted two smashing crisscross blows across the chest from his opponent's whip.

Inside the carriage of William's cab, the drama intensified to the breaking point. Jenny nervously smoked a cigarette while Orville struggled to hold a wrist with a long sharp knife coming through the window on the left, and a second wrist with a long sharp knife coming through the window to the right.

Both gleaming points of the knives were aimed at pretty Jenny's delicious head. She blinked at the knobby fingers holding the honed blades, puffed her cigarette with abandon, and changed her tune:

> "I've got the sweetest
> little dimple
> in my cheek."

On the roof of Finney's cab, Finney and Sigi continued to trade whip blows furiously. Sigi was breathing hard and showed the crimson signs of being slightly cut up. Finney's clothes were practically shredded strips.

During a very brief break in the violent proceedings, Moriarty's henchman looked ahead, down the street. He saw what appeared to be a giant hand hanging out over the sidewalk. As they approached the thing, he could see that it was indeed an enormous wooden hand sticking out from the shop of

HEMMING *The Glovemaker*

Finney grabbed the three-and-a-half-foot hand as the cab passed by it. He smiled at Sigi, triumphantly displaying his awesome new weapon.

The detective quickly looked about him in every direction, searching for a little similar luck—and help. His eyes lit up like beacons when, a few paces farther down the street, he spotted a giant foot. It hung out over the sidewalk, from the shop of

BLAKES *The Bootmaker*

The hansom whizzed by. Sigi grabbed the three-and-a-half-foot foot.

Finney's expression swiftly changed from conceit to concern. With his great "hand," he took a great swipe at Sigi's head. Sigi ducked and cocked his "foot." The next thing Finney knew (the message having been telegraphed by an agonizing pain in his crotch), he had been kicked right in the balls by the giant wooden foot, and was sailing off the roof.

Sigi leapt from the roof of Finney's cab back onto the roof of his own just as William was directing his vehicle into a narrow alley, wide enough for the carriage only.

The two driverless hansom cabs were forced to veer off to the left and to the right—down separate streets.

Finney stumbled onto the cobblestones. Now in total shreds, he slowly began walking. He stepped very carefully, limping slightly, and waved his giant hand in the air.

"Taxi!" he called out in a feeble, soprano voice.

Chapter IX

A WHILE LATER, the ferocious adventure of the carriage race ended (ending, at least for the time being, threat to life and limb), the four-wheeler cab entered a lower-middle-class neighborhood.

The streets were lined with cheap boardinghouses. The cab pulled up and stopped at one of the dreary places. Orville stepped out, followed by Jenny, whom he graciously helped onto the sidewalk. The pensive Sigi chose to remain inside the carriage.

"Jenny, this isn't the way—," Orville said, holding her hand.

"I don't wish to talk about it."

"The problem won't disappear," Sigi ventured from the carriage, "just because you don't wish to talk about it."

"Nevertheless," she maintained, "I don't wish to talk about it."

"You're making a tragic mistake," Orville sadly advised.

"I've made a tragic mistake. More tragic than you can possibly imagine. And unless I'm very careful— I'm going to die for it. I pray you know how grateful I am to both of you. But now I no longer require your services. Please, let me go."

Orville let go of her hand.

"Thank you," she added. "Good night, Sergeant Sacker."

"Good night, Jenny."

The gentle lady walked to the door of the creaky-looking house, took out her key, and opened the door.

She turned back. "Thank you for a lovely evening."
She stepped inside and closed the door behind her.

Orville returned to the carriage. He and his companion looked out the window at Jenny's flat. The
carriage drove off slowly.

"You were very cold, weren't you?" Sacker said.

"Was I?" Sigi asked.

"I thought so. Rather lacking in any emotion, I
should say. The girl was obviously frightened to
death."

"Emotion," Holmes the Philosopher intoned, "is
like one grain of sand in a delicate Swiss watch."

Looking back, they both saw a light go on in Jenny's
room.

"Don't you care for her at all?"

"No!" Sigi maintained, a little more emphatically
than necessary. "But I do care what *happens* to her."

It was long after the departure of Sigi and Orville
that Jenny came out into the street again from her
seedy dwelling. This time, however, she was dressed
elegantly. Gathering the folds of her plush velvet skirt,
she walked hurriedly down the street.

Some time later, the pride of the Tivoli Theatre
walked into another street. The second street, it was
easy to tell, was in an exclusive, well-groomed neighborhood. She walked up to a magnificent town house
and took a key from her purse. After a furtive look
around her, she opened the ornately carved door and
went inside.

If Jenny had looked more slowly and more keenly,
she might have seen a figure standing in the shadows
some short distance away. The shadows, however,
would have precluded her from recognizing the figure:
it was Sigi, who was watching her every move.

The next day, Orville sat in Sigi's room reading the
Morning Post—of Wednesday, April 14, 1891. His
attention was focused on a long article near the center
of the newspaper page that was boldly headlined:

S. HOLMES AVERTS TRAGEDY

Orville began reading the article aloud to the S. Holmes of the headline, who, very nonheroically, was presently stretched out on his bed, in his pajamas, dawdling with a new trusty sword-cane:

" 'Last night, in an unusually brilliant debut, Mr. Holmes not only averted a tragic accident at the Tivoli music hall, but also displayed a charming, if somewhat naïve, musical talent when he "sang" a young artiste away from her position, where, only a few moments later, a prop motorcar slipped from its safety catches and crashed onto the stage. If London rests a bit more securely tonight, it is once again due to Mr. Sherlock—' "

The tip of a sword indelicately interrupted Mr. Sacker's reading by piercing through the newspaper.

Orville's voice trailed off, " '—Holmes, who, in his quiet, unassuming genius . . .' "

Sigi carved a large square out of the center of the paper with the tip of the sword.

"Care for some more tea, Sacker," he asked casually, after having gritted his teeth.

"Yes," Sacker said, staring at Sigi through the hole in his newspaper.

"Make us some, then, would you? The water's boiling."

Orville himself showed some annoyance at the *Morning Post*'s news distortion—assigning Sigi's feat to Sherlock—as he shuffled over to the boiling water.

"What I don't understand," he said, making the tea, "is whether someone was just trying to kill Jenny, or whether someone was trying to kill Jenny because she was with you?"

"What I don't understand," Sigi sighed, "is why Jenny had three different colors of chalk underneath her fingernails."

"Colored chalk under her fingernails?"

"Yes. And that, my boy, is much more to the point."

Orville admitted, "I'm not sure I under—"

"Shhh!" Sigi stopped him and listened to something outside the door. "Hullo!"

"What?" Orville looked confused.

"Shhh!" Sigi again demanded.

"I didn't hear anything," his friend whispered.

"That doesn't necessarily mean that there wasn't anything to hear," Holmes parried. *"Don't run away, Jenny!"* He called at the door. "I assure you there's no cause for embarrassment. Just put your hand back on the doorknob—and walk in!"

The doorknob was turned haltingly. The door opened slowly.

Hunkston, the lumbering porter of Gargantuan hulk, appeared timidly in the doorway.

"Telegram for you, sir," he grunted to Holmes. "Just arrived."

"I thought I told you not to play outside my door," Sigi reminded him.

"Yes, sir. I was only just—"

"Never mind. There's no time for this nonsense. Give the telegram here."

"Yes, sir," Hunkston obeyed. From his gross hand to Sigi's artistic hand, he transferred the cable and clumped out.

Sigi read the cable. He turned his blue eyes to Orville.

"What does it say?" the latter asked, while swilling hot water around in two cups.

Sigi read aloud " 'Greasy goose dressing excellent. Leave room for exactly two servings before theater and pass Redlion on Cheddar Street Cheese.' "

"Interesting," Orville managed, clicking his tongue over the sudden derangement of his new friend. "Well, I really should be going."

"Don't be a ninny!" Sigi snapped. "It's obviously a code of some sort. I just have to decipher it."

"What do you suppose it means?" Orville inquired, as Sigi took a cup from him.

"Cheddar Street Cheese. Cheddar Street Cheese.

Cheddar Street! Is there any street in London by that name?"

"None."

"Curious!" mused the detective, taking a pencil and some paper. "The clue obviously lies in the word 'Cheddar.' Seven letters!" He made some jottings. "Re-arranged, they come out—let me see—red-ched . . . dech-dar . . . drech-ad . . . chad-erd. Hullo! *Chad-erd!* Unless I am very much mistaken, *chad-erd* is the Egyptian word meaning 'to eat fat.' Now we're getting somewhere."

Orville sipped his tea. "Did you try school code?"

"What do you mean?"

"Grammar-school code: count off every third word."

"What are you talking about?" Sigi demanded. "Do you think we're dealing with simpletons? All you'd get from that is—" Sigi looked back at his message and read " 'Dressing room . . . two . . . theater . . . Redlion Street.' "

The youngest of the Holmes boys looked up slowly, silently, trying to conceal his humiliation.

Orville modestly sipped his tea.

Sigi sipped from his cup and immediately spit it out!

"I suppose *you* call this *tea?*" he roared.

"No," Orville, the decoding expert, replied sweetly. "I call it hot water. I was just swilling the water, warming your cup, when you grabbed it."

"May—I—have—some—tea, please?" Sigi ground out, holding back his rage.

"Why, certainly," the obliging Sergeant Sacker replied, and he poured the miffed Mr. Holmes a cup of zesty, delicious, honey-colored tea.

Chapter X

NOTORIOUS PROFESSOR MORIARTY sat behind a small table in his laboratory. He had a gavel in his hand and a sheet of paper, plumed pen, and inkwell in front of him. Finney stood over his right shoulder, somewhat in the manner of an ill-natured pet parrot.

A Russian and a Frenchman, both splendidly outfitted in military dress—citations and polished buttons adorning their manly chests—sat opposite the professor.

"Gentlemen, the Redcliff document will be in my hands at approximately six minutes past ten this evening. What am I bid?" Moriarty addressed the officers in a no-nonsense, all-business, time-is-money manner.

The Russian and the Frenchman exchanged suspicious, military looks.

"Russia bids five thousand," the Russian announced.

Moriarty smiled knowingly at Finney. He began writing, repeating, "Russia bids five thousand—"

"*Rubles!*" the officer from Russia exclaimed.

Moriarty looked up in dismay.

"Well, all right," he muttered and started figuring with pen and paper.

"Let's see. There are, at the current exchange rates, eight rubles to a pound. So! We just put eight into five thousand. Eight into fifty goes six, carrying the two, drop the zero. Eight into twenty is two, carry the four. Eight into forty goes five times. Russia bids *six hundred and twenty-five pounds!* It's a good thing I was a math professor."

57

The mathematical genius laughed his curlicue laugh with satisfaction.

"SEVEN THOUSAND FRANCS!" shouted the Frenchman.

Moriarty gave him a cold, bolt-straight stare.

"Yes. All right," he said, then turned to the ever-present Finney. "Get me today's paper."

Finney produced a paper.

"France bids seven thousand *francs!*" he repeated before muttering under his breath, "What's the franc going for today?"

Finney looked it up. "The franc is—eleven point eighteen!"

"The franc is eleven point eighteen to the pound," the professor summed up. "So! We just put down eleven point eighteen, and—" He turned to his assistant, whispering, "Christ, how do you do this?"

"Did you put down the eleven point eighteen?" Finney whispered back.

"Oh sure, I wouldn't even know to put down the eleven point eighteen," Moriarty whispered again, exasperated. "What I'm askin', ya idiot, is whether ya multiply or divide?"

"Divide."

"Are you sure?"

"Yes."

"I'll kill ya if ya screw this up," Moriarty warned Finney under his breath. Returning to a normal voice, he resumed, "Now, we simply divide seven thousand by eleven point eighteen, and we get— What d'ya do with the decimal point, Mr. Finney?"

"Move it over two places to the right."

"Ya mean I've gotta divide eleven hundred and eighteen into seven thousand?"

"Into seven hundred thousand!" Finney corrected his master.

"Into WHAT?"

"Yu've gotta ad on two zeros to the seven thousand to make up for movin' the decimal point two places to the right on the eleven hundred and eighteen."

"What the hell did we move the decimal point for in the first place?" Moriarty demanded.

"To make it easier," Finney replied flippantly.

The professor slapped Finney in the face. Then, he slapped him in the pride by commanding, "Get the hell out of here!"

While the abused assistant stepped back a few feet, holding his smacked cheek, Moriarty returned to his figures, once again muttering under his breath. "God-damn French bastard."

With still a little more figuring, he turned to the pair in front of him, exclaiming "All right! France bids six thousand and twenty-six pounds."

Finney cautiously returned closer to Moriarty's sacred presence, suggesting, "Six *hundred* and twenty-six pounds."

Slap! Moriarty gave it to Finney again, right across the face, right in view of two foreign guests. No sooner had he delivered the blow than he turned to the competitors. "Six *hundred* and twenty-six pounds."

"Five thousand sixteen rubles," the Russian came back.

"Quit it! That's enough of that!" the frustrated auctioneer shouted. "From now on all bids will be received in pounds."

Another suspicious exchange of glances passed between the Russian and the Frenchman.

"Russia bids one pound."

"One pound, ten shillings," the Frenchman responded.

"Two pounds," the Russian topped him.

"QUIT IT!" came another shout from the professor. "That's enough! The bidding will begin at five thousand pounds."

The Russian and the Frenchman glared at each other.

"Five thousand," the Russian began.

"Eight thousand," bid the Frenchman.

"Ten thousand."

"Twelve thousand."

"Fifteen!"

"Seventeen!"

"Eighteen!"

"Twenty!"

"Twenty-one!"

The bidding continued with progressively increased passion and progressively higher figures. Moriarty turned to Finney and smiled, his avaricious appetite for ill-wrought material gain being pumped into balloon proportions.

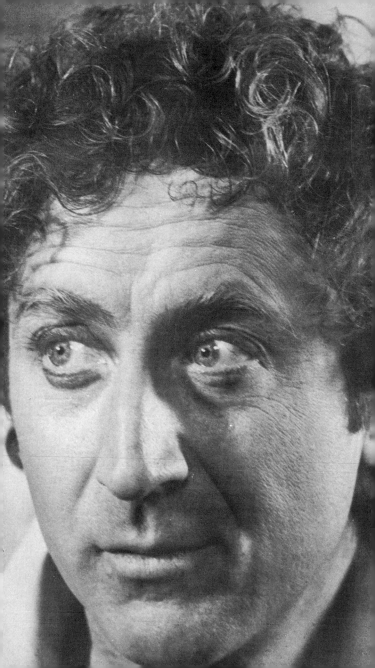

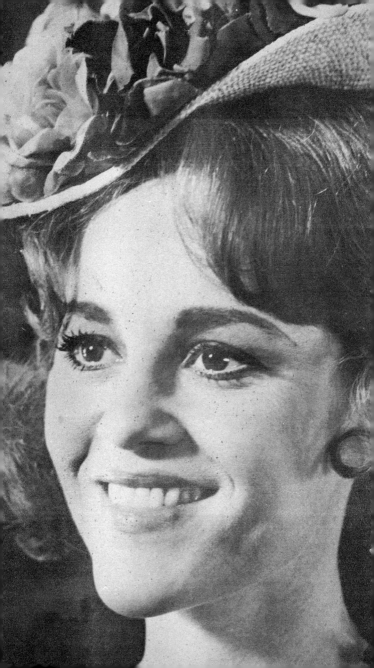

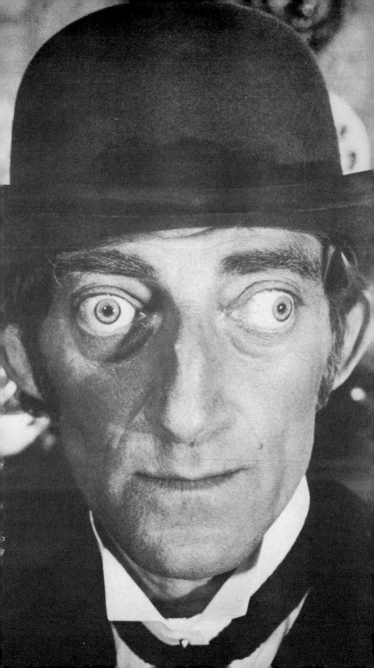

Chapter XI

SIGERSON HOLMES, consulting detective, arrived at the Tivoli Theatre that afternoon, just as the coded telegram had urged him to do. He confidently approached the dressing room of Miss Jenny Hill and rapped upon the dressing-room door.

"Come in!" called a voice that he had begun to find very sweet.

He opened the door with the strength and determination that formed the basis of his character. When he entered the dressing room, however, that self-built strength was more than slightly sapped, and his eyes widened in wonder.

For there was Jenny Hill stretched out on a chaise lounge, wearing only bloomers and bodice, high-heeled shoes, and a choker around her neck. She was sipping a cup of tea and nibbling on a biscuit.

"How good of you to come," said the vision, gently. "May I pour you some tea?"

"Thank you," Sigi politely accepted, trying to act as if all were perfectly normal. He looked quickly around the room, deducing without much delay that no one else was there. The two of them were quite alone. Only some costumes hung on a paneled screen and some cosmetics covered a dressing table.

"Am I interrupting anything?" Sigi asked the singing star as she poured him a stiff cup of tea.

"Not at all. I was just choosing some new costumes for my act. Milk and two sugars?"

"Thank you." He took off his hat.

"Sit down, won't you?" she invited, tapping the chaise.

She offered her guest the cup of tea.

"Thank you," Sigi said, setting down his hat, taking the refreshing tea, and sitting down on the edge of the chaise. "May I ask what made you change your mind about seeing me?"

"Yes, you may."

A dramatic moment of silence was shared.

"What made you change your mind about seeing me?" Sigi asked what he had asked if he could ask.

"I'll tell you something," said the lady. "If you had a stronger chin, you'd be a pretty good looker. What do you think of that?"

"And I'll tell you something," the gentleman countered. "You are a frightened little girl who, for some twisted reason, needs to be sexually excited before she'll trust any living soul with the deepest secrets in her heart. What do you think of that?"

"That is the most ridiculous thing I ever heard in my life."

Sigi placed one of his his hands on Jenny's bountiful breast.

There was another moment of silent anticipation, an interlude during which Holmes sipped his tea with his free hand (his otherwise-occupied hand was much the happier of the two).

Jenny chose to bring the tingling wait to an end, trying with all her being—not to mention her magnificent flesh—to act as if she were *not* physically stimulated. "Ahem! Would you like me to warm your pee? I *mean*—would you like me to warm your *tea?"*

"No, thank you."

"Well, I'm certainly not going to sit here and deny . . ."

"Yes?"

". . . that I'm alarmed by what's happening with my father," she confessed through a deep sigh, and offered her caller a small plate of cookies. "Biscuit?"

"No, thank you." Sigi refused, holding his firm hand

steadily on her breast. "What *is* happening to your father?"

"Well, since I stole that document from his safe . . ."

"Yes?"

". . . he hasn't been the same man."

Jenny now began to speak with more and more genuine sincerity, allowing some of her guilt to pour out. At the same time, she moved her torso a bit to feel more genuinely his stimulating hand on her breast. "I mean, he'll spend an hour just staring off into space. I didn't know that little piece of paper was so important to him."

She lowered her head onto Sigi's solid arm. "I swear I didn't."

"I'm sorry, Jenny. I didn't mean to make you sad. I was only trying . . ." Sigi groped to explain, moved by her sorrow. He removed his hand from her breast.

She sat up, suddenly and straight. "What are you doing?"

"What?"

"What are you taking your hand away for?"

"I wasn't interested in . . ." He groped some more. "I mean, I wasn't even trying to actually— I was just proving a point."

"Oh," she exhaled, not being able to dissemble that she wasn't let down.

"Emotion of that sort is the end to all reason," he continued, trying desperately to hold on to the absolute truth of his grain-of-sand-in-a-delicate-Swiss-watch theory. "I simply can't afford it. It would destroy me."

"I see."

"I'm sorry if I—"

"That's all right."

"Well, perhaps we'd better call it a day," the gentleman concluded, rising and slowly putting on his hat.

Jenny cupped his face in her hands and began to lick his nose and cheeks with the tip of her tongue.

"Don't you want to know about my father?"

"YES!" Sigi was all affirmation at last.

He threw his hat recklessly across the room. He

grabbed Jenny. They kissed long and passionately, falling together onto the chaise lounge.

They kissed again. "For God's sake," said Sigi, coming up for air. "Who is he?"

"I can't tell you *that!*"

"You can't tell me that? That's exactly what you've got to tell me."

Now Sigi took her face into his hands. "Jenny, for once in your life, trust someone!"

"I'm trying. I really am trying." She kissed him again, and followed the lover's seal with "It's very difficult."

He implored. "Jenny, let me help you. Please!"

Miss Hill looked deep into the man's eyes, and started to help him get out of his jacket.

"I will. I will," she promised, succeeding in getting one of his arms out of its jacket sleeve.

"You'll feel better afterward. I promise," he said, struggling to get his other arm free of the jacket.

"I know I will. And you will, too. I promise." She pulled the rest of the jacket off.

"Good! Then who is he?"

"My father?"

"Your father."

"Don't ask."

"Jenny—please," he begged, then kissed her tenderly.

"Oh, Sigi."

"Jenny," he implored compassionately, taking off his tie and shirt, "—who—is—your—father?"

Helping him disrobe between kisses, she began her answer. "He—"

"Good!"

They kissed.

"—is—"

They kissed once more.

"—the—"

"Good!"

"Sigi, I can't."

Sigi promptly shed his pants.

"—*Foreign Secretary for Great Britain!*" she screamed out in a burst of ecstasy.

"Thank you . . . Thank you. Perhaps now we can get to the bottom of things," he whispered, showering her in warmth and lying on top of her.

Chapter XII

SIGI LEFT THE THEATER with his and Jenny's unscheduled performance lingering sweetly and sensually in his mind.

Important business at hand also lingered in his mind. He stopped at a telegraph office. He stopped at his room for a quick change of attire and a cup of tea. In his solitude, he made some favorable mental notes concerning passion and emotion. Then he proceeded directly to the magnificent town house he had seen Jenny go into the night before.

He rang the rich-sounding bell. A most elegant butler opened the sturdy door.

"Mr. Holmes to see Lord Redcliff. I sent a wire."

"Yes, sir," the servant welcomed him. "Won't you come in?"

The butler led Mr. Holmes through the house's large, beautiful reception hall—marble, it was—into Lord Redcliff's stately, imposing study. It was a very formal room that obviously served also as a waiting room for the Foreign Secretary's guests and visiting dignitaries.

"Would you please be seated, sir?" the noble butler implored. "His Lordship will be with you presently."

"Thank you."

The butler left Sigi alone, giving him a chance for a discreet, detailed examination of the study. He viewed the full-length portrait of Lord Redcliff that hung over the mantel. He looked out of a window at the beautiful green grounds.

Many, many things were noted by his precise perception. One of the things noted, sitting on a desk in front of the window, was a lovely box of chocolates with a deliciously ornate cover.

Sigi removed the cover and popped a piece of the candy into his mouth. It was marvelous-tasting, but the chocolate had become very runny, having sat in the day's hot sun. The detective licked his fingers, and took one more irresistible chocolate.

Upon giving in to his desire for a third piece of this wonderfully rich candy, the poor man accidentally knocked the candy off the desk, spilling the melted pieces of the rich brown confection all over the floor.

Naturally embarrassed, Sigi scrambled to pick up the chocolates and stuff them back into the box.

He was contemplating the awful, gooey mess that covered his right hand when, alas, Lord Redcliff made his untimely appearance.

"Mr. Holmes!" the distinguished gentleman intoned.

Mr. Holmes rapidly stuffed the chocolates remaining in his hands into the only available receptacle—his smart mouth. He rose and turned to face his Lordship with as much dignity as he could salvage while hiding the box of chocolates in his left hand behind his back.

Lord Redcliff witnessed, as could only be expected, a caller with an outrageously messy brown mouth.

"Lord Redcliff, I presume," Sigi slurped through a mouth full of candy.

Lord Redcliff approached him hesitantly, stating, "I can't tell you how glad I am to see you."

The great man extended his hand.

"How very nice of you to say," Sigi acknowledged his welcome and shook the famous hand before him.

His Lordship felt something gooey on his hand. He snuck a glance down at the hand, to discover it, too, was brown from chocolate.

"Did you find out anything?" the good man asked, holding back his suspicions out of his respect for his visitor.

"Many things! Many things!" Sigi replied, still struggling to speak understandably with a full mouth.

"I mean about—" Lord Redcliff stopped himself to switch to another question. "You are Mr. Holmes, aren't you?"

"Yes, that's right."

During the exchange, Sigi successfully fixed the lid back on the candy box behind his back and replaced the chocolates to their original position on the desk.

Lord Redcliff resumed. "Mr. *Sherlock* Holmes?"

"No, I'm his brother—Sigerson."

"Sigerson?" the confused lord inquired, surreptitiously licking the chocolate from his fingers.

"As I'm sure you're aware," Sigi stated, also licking chocolate from his fingers, "my brother comes to me for help on many of his more difficult cases."

Lord Redcliff licked some more chocolate from his hand and abruptly forced a turn in the interview. "What is it you wish of me, Mr. Holmes? I am a very busy man."

"No more busy than I, your Lordship, I assure you," Sigi insisted, by then fully occupied with licking sweet goo from his fingers.

"Well, then, come to the point!"

"The point is, Lord Redcliff, that your daughter told me everything."

"My daughter!?" Lord Redcliff's eyebrows ascended almost past his hairline and he took an expansively long step toward his visitor. "Would you mind telling me, sir, how you could possibly know my daughter?"

"I have saved her life on two separate occasions."

"May I ask where and when?"

"Last night, at the Tivoli music hall, and then later in a four-wheeler near Piccadilly Circus."

"I see. Would you mind describing her to me?"

"If you think that's necessary, certainly. She has magnificent red hair, about twenty-seven years of age, I should say five feet four inches tall—and extraordinarily beautiful."

"Would you please leave my house, sir," the imposing personage requested of his now unwanted guest.

"But," stammered Sigi, "I don't understand. What have I said?"

"Mr. Holmes, or whoever you are," Lord Redcliff sternly addressed him, "my daughter has blonde hair, she is a little under five feet, and she is *twelve years of age.*"

"I—"

"Since my wife died, five months ago, I have sent my daughter to boarding school in Reading, and I have lived here with my two other children—both boys—ages five and six. Would you please leave my house?"

"But the paper, sir," Sigi protested.

"What paper?"

"Well, I mean, wasn't there an important paper stolen from your wall safe?"

"Most certainly not," Lord Redcliff stated, taking out a pocket watch from the pocket of his superbly cut suit. "I'll give you exactly sixty seconds to leave this house, and then I shall call the police."

Sigi, confounded as he was, didn't need the allotted sixty seconds. He walked quickly out of the study, Lord Redcliff following him. At the end of the reception hall, the butler already had the front door open, awaiting his exit into the ever-puzzling world.

The sleuth with infallible instincts looked furtively for any clues he might find, a flash search covering Lord Redcliff's face, the butler's face, and the walls of the hall. He stepped through the front doorway of the magnificent town house.

"Good day, sir," was the butler's final remark, and the door was firmly shut.

Sigerson was in utter bewilderment, a state of existence most unusual for him. He stood on the town-house front steps for a moment, absentmindedly licking the last of the chocolate from his fingers.

Finally descending those steps, he turned up the street. A pensive mood engulfed him as he walked. His train of thought stopped when he suddenly heard a harmonica playing "The Kangaroo Hop."

Motionless, he listened to the music. He rapidly glanced around, to see a street entertainer playing the tune that now had such a special meaning for him. He turned back, walking toward the musician and listening to his music.

Standing on the sidewalk opposite Lord Redcliff's mansion, he surveyed the third floor, then the fourth floor, and finally the slanted roof.

He crossed the street and, from the grounds at one side of the mansion, he began to climb.

When he reached the top of the house, he stretched out precariously across the sloping roof until he could peer into a fourth-floor window.

There, in what obviously was a children's classroom, was *Jenny Hill!*

She was drawing, and filling in—with colored chalk —sections of a map of the British Isles on a blackboard. Two young boys, about five and six years old, sat at little desks watching her and copying her map into their notebooks. She was talking and they were talking, although, of course, the rooftop observer could not make out what they were saying.

Soon, Lord Redcliff entered the room. His two small sons put down their notebooks and jumped into their father's arms. He hugged them. He put them down. The Foreign Secretary shook the governess's hand. He spoke to the boys, motioning toward the door, and the bright, well-mannered youngsters bounced out of the room.

Lord Redcliff walked to the door, closed it, and returned to Jenny Hill, or rather, bounced back to her, with a lilt quite light for his age. He took her in his arms and they kissed passionately.

So shocked and so distressed was Sigi Holmes at what he had seen, he lost his footing on the clifflike roof and began to slide down.

He slid *down* the roof, *off* the roof, and helplessly sailed through the air, along the path of a rain pipe. He landed—SPLAT!—into a huge barrel filled with water.

There was no sign whatsoever of the detective for an uncomfortably long time, during which his hat floated on top of the water. Then he emerged slowly from the rain barrel, his hat, amazingly still on his head. He climbed out of his soggy confinement, shook his feet, shivered throughout his body, and began his damp return-trip home.

When he was safely back on the sidewalk, a very proper lady, out for a relaxing stroll, approached from the opposite direction. The equally proper Mr. Holmes was compelled to straighten his dripping tie. As the lady passed, he raised his hat, valiantly attempting to assume a drop of dignity in his wet clothing.

Water poured from his hat onto and thoroughly over his head. His dignity drowned; his stature shrunk to a puddle.

Chapter XIII

IT WAS ONE of those lush day-to-remember days.

The sun sprinkled brightly through the trees in one of the prettiest parks on the outskirts of London. The breeze gently ruffled the leaves on the branches.

Along a beautiful, secluded walk, Sigi and Jenny moved in silence. Orville trailed a short distance behind them.

Sigi tossed a thought or two about in his head. At last he spoke to the woman at his side. "If this isn't the truth, I shall never speak to you again. I swear it."

"This is the truth: Lord Redcliff is my fiancé."

Sigi looked deep into her eyes. Orville looked at her, his eyes deeply startled.

"I've been governess in his home for three years," Jenny explained. "Lady Redcliff was dying during the last two. I thought at first he wanted me only for the sake of his children. But, when his wife died, I realized it was more than that. He really does love me. We were going to be married this very Friday afternoon. But now——"

"How *could* you have stolen that document from him?" Sigi demanded.

"I didn't know what was in it. I still don't. It was just politics, that's all. Rotten, insensitive, smelly politics."

"So you stole the document and gave it to Gambetti?" Sigi wanted her to reaffirm her story.

"Yes," she said.

"And now Gambetti won't give you back your love letter."

"No. He gave it back when I gave him the document."

Sigi, surprised once more, stopped her.

"Then what in God's name do you want from me?"

"I want you to steal the document back from Gambetti."

Sigi looked up to the sky, then across to Orville, and back to Jenny. "Where would you like us to drop you off?" he asked with some exasperation.

"He's going to resign as Foreign Secretary," she informed her escorts.

"Where would you like us to drop you off?"

"I'm not proud of what I did," she volunteered.

"Ho!" Sigi trumpeted. "You have just told us a magnificent success story. Overlooking the fact that you are a liar, a thief, a traitor, and a whore—I don't see what should be bothering you."

Jenny slapped Sigi's face. She slapped it over and over with one hand. The victim of her fury didn't even try to protect himself; nor did he when she segued into pounding his chest with her fists. She pounded until she was exhausted. It was then that her head drooped to Sigi's shoulder and she wept softly.

"Please help me," she pleaded.

"Do you know where Gambetti lives?" Holmes asked, after a long pause.

"I've been rehearsing in his house for three weeks," Jenny informed him. "Completely innocent of this mess, Lord Redcliff arranged for me to be in Gambetti's opera company. That's the irony: he's been trying to help me with my career since I first met him. He loves my voice."

"Does he know you sing in a music hall?"

"No. He wouldn't like that."

"Pity. Sacker—" He turned to Orville. "We're going to need a floor plan of Gambetti's house. Can you dig one up?"

"Well . . ." Orville reflected.

"I have one in my purse," said Jenny.

". . . Yes, I can." Orville smiled, taking the floor

plan from Jenny, observing how sweetly her face remained buried in Sigi's shoulder.

A small assortment of birds chirped cheerfully.

That night, two masked men, in tails and top hats, ran toward a moon-splashed, six-foot garden wall. They peered over the top.

"So far so good," said Sigi, the masked man on the left.

"I still don't see why the tails and top hats," sighed Orville, the second masked man, who also carried a lantern.

"Simplicity itself!" the consulting detective counseled. "This way, we'll blend in casually with the returning theater and opera crowds afterward."

"Afterward?"

"After we have finished our business."

They climbed over the wall, with a struggle-born grunt here and there, and lowered themselves down the other side. They discovered themselves to be on luxurious property.

Orville cocked his ear. "Do you hear music?"

Sigi could faintly hear an orchestra playing in the distance. "Must be a party going on."

"Might prove a little sticky," Sacker suggested.

"All the better!" his companion assured him. "Something to distract them while we are busy burgling Gambetti's safe."

The raiders hurriedly crept across the lawn.

They surveyed. They surmised. And they succeeded in entering the grand Gambetti home.

In a small hallway, Sigi pulled out the floor plan. Orville opened a shutter of his lantern to give Holmes some reading light.

Sigi pointed. "This way." They stole to Gambetti's great study, opened the door, and stared in.

A crackling fire illuminated the baroquely decorated room. French windows, with curtains on both sides and through which the music of a small orchestra continued to be heard, looked out onto the garden.

Sigi and Orville tiptoed in. Their eyes showed excitement when they spotted the brass knobs of a safe flashing in the firelight.

Holmes deftly closed the door. They slithered to the safe. Sigi stiffly extended his arms and Orville, with professional expertise, helped his partner off with his tool-laden coat, laying it over a chair.

Sigi pulled out two drills, a jimmy, a pair of pliers, and a calibrated wrench. He handed the collection to his colleague. Orville, in turn, carried the tools to the safe and laid them out on the study floor.

Sigi knelt at the safe, a rubber hammer and a rubber chisel now in his hands.

"I'll show you how simple this can be when you know what you're doing," he bragged.

However, the execution of the boast had to be deferred when they heard the humming of a man's voice. The sound came from the hallway, toward them.

"Quick, my coat!" Sigi commanded.

Orville rushed to the chair over which Sigi's coat was draped. He grabbed it, holding it while Sigi stuffed the tools back into the pockets.

"Over here!" Sigi directed, snatching the lantern and blowing it out.

The pair of intruders darted behind the curtains at Gambetti's French windows, Orville on one side, Sigi on the other. Orville rolled the cumbersome overcoat with all the heavy equipment up into his arms.

They stood as still as two owls, and, while the fire in the study crackled, they tried to breathe as silently as two butterflies.

Chapter XIV

EDUARDO GAMBETTI, a fat, bald-headed impresario of Roman ancestry, burst into his study. He was dressed elegantly in tails and sported a slick, black toupee.

He posed in the middle of the room, tears in his eyes, then crossed to the mantelpiece and proceeded to pour out a tragedy-shrouded native lament.

"Dio buono dammi la luce. La donna—la donna non me vuole baciare."

He hit his fist against the mantel.

"Per me la vita é finita!—"

He spotted a dagger on his desk.

"Ecco, il coltello!"

He picked up the dagger and examined it.

"Cosa penserebbe Mamma di questo coltello—"

He spotted his mother's framed photograph on his desk, and spoke to it with passion.

"Mamma! Cosa pensi di questo coltello?"

He kissed the photo.

"Mamma! Addio!"

He raised the gleaming knife, aiming it at his heavy breast.

"Fa presto! Perche io non voglio scomparire—non voglio scomparire—"

(Behind the curtains, Sigi and Orville gazed at each other with increasing alarm.

Sigi was sufficiently aware of Gambetti's native tongue to know that he had ranted something close to: A lady's not wanting to kiss him . . . His life was over . . . A knife . . . Mama . . . Good-bye. And then that he seemed to be stammering, almost as if he were unsure of what to say next.

What he could not see was that Gambetti was now referring to an open opera score on his desk, having forgotten the last line of his monologue. Not being able to see the opera score, Sigi and Orville were unaware that the raving fat man was not in earnest, but in rehearsal.)

Gambetti snapped the opera score shut. "—*non voglio scomparire.*"

With a gesture becoming his flamboyant nature, he scooped up a previously poured drink. He gulped it down and threw the glass into the fireplace. "That's a beauty!"

There came a tapping at the French doors. The opera lover strode to the doors and looked out of one of the squares of glass. He opened the curtains halfway, leaving Sigi and Orville both praying that he didn't look to the left or to the right, for both were then well within his sight range.

Gambetti was occupied, however, waving to someone outside. "Peek and boo!"

Immediately, he unlocked the center doors. There stood Professor Moriarty, decked out in two of his trademarks—a wide-brimmed hat and a cape.

"Professore!" Gambetti gushed, spreading his arms in a grand expanse of welcome.

Moriarty extended his hand. "Signor Gambetti."

The fat man pushed the professor's hand aside and took hold of his face.

"I love-a you hat," he chirped. "I love-a you face. I love-a you nose. Where you keep you wallet?"

"Here," said Moriarty, touching his breast pocket.

Gambetti covered his visitor's hand with his own hand and let out an Italian sound of guttural ecstasy. He kissed Moriarty on the temple.

"You may come inna my house."

The professor walked in, swiftly wiping off Gambetti's lush kiss while his host closed the door—and the curtains.

Moriarty took an envelope from his breast pocket and threw it toward the desktop. Before the packet could land, Gambetti caught it, opened it, and smelled inside. He took out a large bundle of money.

"É squisito!" he chortled, slapping Moriarty in the stomach with the wad of notes.

The impresario sat down at his desk, and with unabashed glee, began counting the money. *"Uno—due —tre—"*

The professor silently gnashed his teeth until his irritation overwhelmed him. He put his hand firmly in the middle of the money.

"Feel free to count it," he intoned sarcastically.

"Don' toucha da money," Gambetti warned, banging Moriarty's hand. *"—quattro—cinque—"* And he was back to the delight of counting the money.

Moriarty stood in agitation. He noticed two large, magnificent vases on the desk. He took one of the *objets d'art* into his hands and raised it slowly over Gambetti's head, moaning softly. "Aaaah!"

The money counter looked up, interrupting his addition.

Moriarty, vase above his head, slid into a compliment. "You've got a lovely vase."

Gambetti, touched, reached up with his right hand and squeezed his guest's cheeks. "And *you* got a lovely vase," he said sweetly, returning the compliment.

"YUH!" Moriarty yelped, lowering the vase, while his muscles twitched.

Gambetti looked up again, in time to catch another weird "YUH!," which was slightly louder this time, as Moriarty came closer to cracking.

"YUH!" Gambetti decided to repeat after his guest. "Hey, we havin' a nice time, huh?"

He slapped Moriarty's stomach again with the wad of notes and stood. "Okay! Correct! Fifty thousand pounds. Signor Moriarty, you mamma raise a nize boy."

(Sigi somewhat suffocating behind the curtain, jerked his head back in amazement when he heard the word *Moriarty*.)

"Now may I have the document?" the professor asked.

Gambetti replaced the money in the envelope and walked to his gleaming safe. *"Scusi,* Professore, *un momento."* He indicated a chair. "Make yourself comfortable. I'll be only one minute."

He sang gaily as he put the bundle of money into his safe:

> "First you had the money.
> Now I got the money.
> Now the money's safe with me."

He snapped the safe securely shut, and turned, full of sweetness, back to the professor. "Now! What you say, Professore?"

"I said: May I have the document?"

Tension sprang forth and consumed the air as Gambetti and Moriarty faced one another across the desk.

"You think I'm crazy?" yelled the Italian, and he slapped Moriarty's face. "You think I keep the document here?"

Moriarty had some difficult time controlling himself. "What did ya say?"

(Sigi and Orville, meanwhile, were listening with all their might from behind the curtains.)

"I say," Gambetti nastily retorted, "I don't keep the document in my house."

The professor began to twitch with both eyes.

(Orville gasped silently as he saw a wrench about to fall out of the coat he held bunched in his arms. He prevented the disaster just in the nick of time.)

"Professore," Gambetti said, "You are a very big man." He poured himself a glass of wine. "If I give you this document tonight"—he tapped Moriarty's chin—"you got many big boys who crack-a my head"—he beat the professor on the head—"and take alla this money back before I send home to Mamma."

The bulky sentimentalist caressed the frame of his mamma's picture. "I thing it's better I give you this document in public. *Salute."* And he drained his glass of wine.

The sound of a drill falling to the floor cracked through the room. But the evil conspirators were too enraptured with their nefarious plans and their gripping competition to take notice.

The professor now twitched continuously and uncontrollably. "In *public?*" he asked. "You want to give me the document in *public?*"

"Si," Gambetti answered.

"Yuh!" Moriarty muttered.

"Yuh!" Gambetti imitated him .

"Yuh!" Moriarty upped the volume.

"Yuh!" Gambetti imitated both the sound and the volume.

"YUH!" Moriarty screamed, turning away from his adversary and bending his knees in frustrated anger.

"YUH!" Gambetti returned.

"YUH! YUH!" Moriarty doubled his fury.

"YUH! YUH!" Gambetti met the challenge.

Moriarty held Gambetti's face. "How the hell are you goin' to give it to me in public?"

Gambetti held Moriarty's face. "In the opera!"

Moriarty twisted Gambetti's ear. "Ya want to give it to me in an OPERA!?"

Gambetti twisted Moriarty's ear. *"Si."*

Moriarty twisted Gambetti's other ear. "WHAT OPERA?"

Gambetti twisted Moriarty's other ear. "ITALIAN!"

Moriarty pulled Gambetti's toupee. "WHICH ITALIAN!"

Gambetti threw Moriarty's hat from his head. *"Un Ballo in Maschera!* By VERDI!"

Moriarty bit Gambetti's fingers. "AND HOW THE HELL DO I GET THE DOCUMENT?"

Gambetti bit Moriarty's fingers. "IT'S EASY!"

Moriarty picked up one of the priceless vases from the desk and smashed it to the floor.

"YUH!"

Gambetti grabbed the second priceless vase and smashed it to the floor.

"YUH!"

Moriarty, breathing very hard, collapsed in a chair.

Gambetti poured himself a glass of wine and sang out, "I AM HAPPY!"

The maestro sat on the edge of his comrade's chair, put his arm around him, and gave him a drink of wine.

"We havin' a nice time, eh?" The gracious host nudged his guest.

"Yuh!" was the soft, exhausted reply.

"How you feel?"

"It's all right," Moriarty answered. "The crisis is over. I feel better now."

The opera manager rose, taking up a pitcher of water from a small table behind the professor.

"Good! I'm glad," he said, pouring water into his glass. "Hey, we have some fun, huh?" He leaned over the emotionally exhausted Moriarty, inadvertently pouring water down the poor man's neck.

"A little expensive, but lots of fun."

Gambetti skipped to an inordinately wide chaise lounge, on which there were two pillows and a patchwork coverlet.

"You were sayin'?" Moriarty prodded him, mopping himself with a handkerchief.

"In the third act," Gambetti began, "the messenger, he sing 'Why don't we all drink some very sexy wine?' "

The professor shook his head, joined Gambetti at the chaise lounge and lay down next to him. Both adjusted themselves into reclining comfort.

"Some very sexy wine? What the hell is that?"

"We don't sing in Italian," the former Roman explained. "We gonna sing the opera in English and I make my own translation 'cause you can't see the real meaning from some words—it doesn't make sense. So I fix 'em up a little."

"Go on."

"When the messenger sing 'Why don't we all drink

some very sexy wine?,' Riccardo—that's-a me—I give him a big piece of paper. Ordinary, it's-a nothing inside. Just a prop."

"Would ya get to the point!"

"*You* send *you own* messenger. He sing 'Why don't we all drink some very sexy wine?' I give him the Red- cliff document instead of the empty prop paper. And everybody happy."

(Sigi was implanting that information into the soil of his brain when a pair of pliers slipped out of the stuffed coat Orville clutched, and fell to the floor.)

Moriarty and Gambetti directed their eyes toward the French-door curtains.

There was the sound of what could have been a wrench falling. There was the sound of what could have been a chisel falling. Finally, there were the sounds of a mass of tools clunking in rapid succession to the floor, and of breaking glass.

Moriarty sprang to his feet and pulled out a small pistol. He shushed Gambetti and crept to the French doors. Quickly, he pulled the cord on the right side, completely opening the right curtain. Orville was ex- posed, unmasked, stuck in the window through which he had just crashed.

"Who the hell are ya?" the professor demanded, with a look alone that could kill.

"Glass fitter," Orville tried. "I was told you needed several new panes of glass for this door. I was just ex- amining it as you came by."

"And do ya always wear formal dress on the job?" the ever-alert Moriarty asked.

" 'Elite Glass for Any Class,' " Sacker offered.

"Is that a fact?"

"You bet your ass."

There was a loud crash!—and the crinkling of glass —from behind the left curtain.

"Ah!" Orville suggested. "That'll be my assistant."

Moriarty went directly to the left side of the doors and pulled the curtain cord. The curtain opened, re- vealing Sigi, sprawled out after having fallen through the glass door behind him. Unlike Orville, he still was masked.

Orville spoke across the doors. "Well, William, if you've made the estimates, we can toddle off now."

"What's happenin'?" Gambetti questioned. "What the hell is goin' on?"

Professor Moriarty moved up to Sigi, motioning with his pistol for him to stand. He removed the mask.

"Good evenin', Mr. Holmes."

"Oy yoy!" Gambetti emitted, pierced by the name and holding his heart.

"Not that one," Moriarty informed his partner. "It's his younger brother."

He addressed the younger brother. "Enjoyin' the entertainment, are ya?"

"First rate!" Sigi replied. "The clowns leave something to be desired, but perhaps I'm being picayune."

"Would you have any absolutely first-rate quarters for our two friends, Signor Gambetti? Where no one could possibly disturb them?"

"Well," thought the master of the house, "I got the guest room. It's a little bit small, but it's very, very private."

Sigi and Orville tried to decline the hospitality. To no avail.

Chapter XV

SIGI AND ORVILLE found themselves in a most undesirable predicament.

It was this: they faced the wall of a long, unbelievably narrow room—the accommodation was, in fact, a mere fifteen inches wide; at one end of the unusual room stood a mighty buzz saw; and, running along the length of the floor, there was a unique drainage system —for blood, no doubt.

Gambetti and Moriarty, witnessing the scene through an open, small metal door, laughed hysterically. Then Gambetti whispered something in Moriarty's ear and the two men laughed even more.

Gambetti turned a switch. The mighty buzz saw ROARED! It revolved at an amazingly high speed, accompanied by a solid ZZZZZZZZZZZZZ, and moved slowly and precisely along the middle of the room toward those most unfortunate of men—Holmes and Sacker.

"Good night," Gambetti crooned to the two victims. "I love you both. Don't have bad dreams."

He clunked the metal door closed.

"I am very frightened," Orville admitted.

The buzz saw picked up forward speed in its passage toward them, intending to make two halves out of each one of them.

"Nothing is hopeless," said Sigi. "Do you understand? Nothing!"

"Thank you. I feel so much better," Orville feigned, giving his partner a stare.

"What in Christ's name did Gambetti just tell Moriarty?" Sigi wondered.

"Professore," Orville said in an Italian accent, "this room is-a fifteen inch wide. My little saw is-a gonna come right down the middle. I hope-a you like the color red."

Sigi looked at him in wonderment.

"I forgot to tell you, I read lips," Orville explained.

"Right down the middle." Sigi pondered Gambetti's words, and his saw. "That means seven and a half inches on either side. Hullo! Our inflated bodies are about eleven inches thick. But without air in them, they should be only seven inches thick—give or take an inch."

"An *inch?*" cried Orville as he looked down in panic.

"Yes. Now, then—when I say so, start exhaling. But not before I say so or you might be forced to in-hale while the saw is still on you. Do you understand?"

"Yes."

The saw was by then horrendously close to them. It was gleaming with sharpness.

"Get ready," Sigi instructed. *"Now!"*

They flattened themselves out against the wall and exhaled with all their might.

ZZZZZZZZZZZZZZZZ came the saw.

Eureka! Sigi's ingenious method worked. The saw passed by them both, along their backs. They desperately held their breath until the saw passed them completely. Then they inhaled like crazy.

When the saw had passed their bodies, however (unbeknownst to the two men—so sharp were the teeth and so relieved were they to be alive), it had shaved all the clothes off their backsides. Right off, from their shoulders to the backs of their shoes.

Although they remained fully dressed in front, two rosy tushies were fully exposed to all the world.

"This way, quickly!" Sigi ordered, and they rushed to the point from which the buzz saw had started its journey. There was an air shaft going up.

"I knew the gear shaft would have to lead either up or down," Sigi bragged, starting to climb up. "With any luck, this should see us safely onto the streets of London."

At the end of their upward journey, Sigi and Orville were looking through a ventilator. Their four eyes moved from side to side, surveying the surroundings.

They had not reached the streets of London. They had reached, rather, an empty bathroom, a Ladies' Bathroom. They put their fingers through the grill-work, pushed the ventilator onto the floor and crawled out of the air shaft, into the bathroom.

They opened a door, the only door available to them, and walked into the Ladies' Powder Room.

The powder room at that moment happened to be rather crowded, with seven lovely damsels touching up the make-up on their faces on both sides of the room. All of the occupants turned toward the intruders in surprise, which transformed itself into angry shock at the realization that two *men* had just emerged from the Ladies' Bathroom.

Sigi and Orville faced the ladies and the situation bravely. They assumed a supersophisticated stance, both still innocent of the fact that their backsides were unclothed.

"Good evening, ladies," Sigi saluted.

"Lovely party. Excellent wine," Orville commented agreeably.

The two men walked toward the double-door exit. When they passed the ladies, the naked splendor of their fully exposed tushies was too much for the assembly of poor women to take. The group gasped in unison. Then, one by one, the women fainted.

The sound of collapsing bodies forced the two men to turn around at the same moment. They witnessed seven unconscious female forms sprawled about all over the powder-room floor.

"Strange," was how Sigi summed it up.

"I wonder what's got into them?" Orville puzzled.

"Never mind! Let's get out of here."

Through the double doors, the escapees walked into a ballroom filled with dancing couples. One wall was composed partially of mirrors. A huge candelabrum lit the room. A compact orchestra played a mazurka. And a wide assortment of ladies and gentlemen, all elegantly dressed, were dancing-talking-eating-drinking.

Momentarily shocked by their new circumstances, Sigi and Orville stood motionless. Then they summoned up the nerve required to do what they must: act out the game—walk into the room and join the crowd.

They nodded greetings to dancing couples and groups of revelers. Before they knew what had happened, however, they found themselves part of a single line of men that faced a single line of women.

The tempo and the volume of the music heightened. The line of men danced the mazurka to the left; the women danced to the right. After that, the men turned their backs to the women and mazurka'd in the opposite direction.

Couples began to freeze on the dance floor. Mouths dropped in horror. Bodies went limp. Hair stood on some heads. The eyes of many women nearly popped out of their sockets. Petrification occupied the ballroom as more and more guests were treated to a spectacular view of the birthday-suit backsides of Mr. Holmes and Mr. Sacker.

Finally, some God-granted, self-preserving instinct made Sigi and Orville turn their heads to the mirror at the same time. They flushed with panic at the sign of their bare flesh. Their panic prompted them to leap at two nearby ladies and dance them around the room frantically.

Several of the more decorous females present screeched loud screams!

Sigi and Orville left their reluctant partners, clasped hands, and danced—back to back—toward the ballroom's front window, smiling at the crowd all through their ordeal. When they reached the window, they dove through the glass, performed a swinging somersault on the lawn, and raced toward, at last, the streets of London.

The ladies and gentlmen in Gambetti's ballroom stared after them, mesmerized by the pair of naked behinds disappearing into the darkness.

Chapter XIII

Chapter XVI

ON A NIGHT marked for history, the score of a noted opera was being painstakingly studied in a number of locations all over London.

Sigi read the musical notes in his room while, behind him, Orville tied his black tie.

Jenny, her hair up in curlers and expertly applying make-up in her dressing-room mirror, also had the open score in front of her.

Gambetti perused the opera's pages in his mammoth "star" dressing room. He was in make-up, half-costumed, and wearing a wig of black curls. The pages were blotched with red, for he refused to put down his meatball sandwich, from which marinara sauce rhythmically dripped, while studying the notes.

Moriarty, in his laboratory, came to the part in the score that read "Cymbals," and responded by crashing the pair of cymbals he held in his hands. Moriarty's companion, the famous marksman Colonel von Stulberg—his asthmatic breathing almost metronomic—sat nearby cleaning his air gun.

And finally, in another residential room—on Baker Street—puffs of smoke clung to the score as it was being memorized by a tall, slender man smoking an *enormous, drooping pipe*. Behind him stood a stout man tying the pipe smoker's black tie.

The orchestra sat in readiness in the pit of Saint Timothy's Hall. The large, formally attired audience had partially settled down, waiting for the performance.

The cover of the evening's program, a program preserved to this day in a Scotland Yard bin of memorabilia, read:

"A MASKED BALL"
by
Giuseppe Verdi

ENGLISH TRANSLATION
by
EDUARDO GAMBETTI

The hall's backstage was a cacophony of movement and voices. The area was packed with opera singers wearing little black masks. Some of the performers had their masks in position, others had them pushed back on their foreheads.

Most of them were limbering up their vocal cords. "Aah . . . Aah" and "Mii . . . Mii" rang out in profusion. They were dressed as ladies and gentlemen of the eighteenth-century Swedish court of Gustav III, as the setting of the Verdi opera demanded. Almost every man sported a sword.

The area was filled also with prop tables and wardrobe racks. On one of the prop tables—the one most pertinent to the Gambetti-Moriarty scheme—rested five identical rolls of parchment, each document tied with a blue ribbon.

In the center of the teeming place, two masked messengers surveyed the scene. They were fully costumed. They were Sigi and Orville.

"Keep your ears open for an Irish accent," said the masked Sigi.

"Right!" Orville signaled, and they walked off in

different directions, each warming up their singing prowess.

Meanwhile, in the auditorium of the hall, the orchestra had just begun the overture.

In the half-dim house, Lord Redcliff was seated in his box.

Moriarty was seated in his box, spying on Lord Redcliff with binoculars. Colonel von Stulberg, carrying his unusual and lethal cane, was seated with the professor.

Moriarty, in turn, was being spotted through binoculars. His observers were the high-bidding Russian and French military officers who were vying to purchase the Foreign Secretary's stolen document. Now they were sharing a box, warmly enjoying each other's company.

The overture ended. The audience applauded. The conductor bowed.

Eduardo Gambetti stood in the stage-left wings, gargling. Once his throat was refreshed, he swallowed and held out his tulip-shaped glass, which a stagehand promptly filled with more full-bodied, deep-red wine.

From the prop table a hand lifted one of the blue-ribboned documents. Four of its counterparts remained.

Jenny, magnificent in her costume, still sat in front of her dressing-room mirror, applying the last touches of her make-up. She pressed her hand against her breast to calm the hard pounding of her heart.

Sigi and Orville, in their masks, had rejoined one another and were standing in the stage-right wings, surrounded by masked singers.

The conductor signaled his orchestra. The houselights went down from half dim to out. The conductor, his face illuminated by the petite light on his music stand, raised his baton and waited for complete silence.

The audience—including the aforementioned Lord Redcliff, Moriarty, Colonel von Stulberg, Russian, and Frenchman—turned its attention to the stage.

The conductor gave the downbeat with his baton. The glorious music began.

The great landmark clock atop Saint Timothy's Hall sang its own tune of the hour.

The curtain rose for the premiere performance of Eduardo Gambetti's version of Verdi's *A Masked Ball* at 8:00 P.M.—precisely as scheduled.

Chapter XVII

THE CURTAIN CAME DOWN on the second act of Eduardo Gambetti's version of Verdi's *A Masked Ball* a little before 9:45.

By that time, Colonel von Stulberg, Moriarty's weapon-toting companion, had his air gun fully assembled and resting against his seat in the box.

There was a brief intermission. Some members of the audience strolled up and down the aisles of Saint Timothy's Hall. A bell recalled them to their seats.

The music for the final act began. The curtain rose.

The stage had been magically transformed into a palatial grand ballroom. It was filled with masked singers, who counted among their number Sigi and Orville.

The set glittered, the music swelled. And the chorus sprang forth with some more of the new, Gambetti-fashioned libretto set to Verdi's immortal music:

> "We're singing at a party.
> We ate a great big dinner.
> Hot *hors-d'oeuvres!*
> Cold *hors-d'oeuvres!*
> Boy, did we stuff ourselves.
> The chicken was delicious.
> And now we'll all start dancing.
> Up and down! All around!
> Let's hope we don't get sick!"

The singers danced a little dance, at the end of which, as one body, they looked upstage.

Gambetti and Jenny, who was masked, made their grand entrance as the opera's Riccardo and Amelia. Into

95

Gambetti's belt was stuffed a rolled-up document tied with a blue ribbon.

Jenny, as is written in *A Masked Ball,* covered her face with a fan.

Gambetti, pulling her fan away, sang:

> "Hey!
> You cannot hide that angel face.
> I knew you by the smell."

From his box, through his binoculars, Professor Moriarty spotted the document in the fat man's belt. He sucked in a greedy breath of air.

Jenny-Amelia, coyly holding on to her fan, sang to Gambetti:

> "Stop that
> —you're such a tickle tease.
> You know
> —I'm superpassionate.
> Oh my, you make my heart go ZOW.
> Try to hold on to your sex urge.
> I won't . . .
> I can't sleep over.
> (*He touched her face. She sighed.*)
> All right
> —I'll try it once.
> If I see that it doesn't work,
> I'll know that *then*
> Maybe
> practice
> would
> help."

"Curious translation," a lady in the audience opined aloud. Several of the members of the elegant assemblage agreed with her. Further than that—such as deciding whether the whole thing was blatantly rotten or wonderfully brave—they were unwilling to go until they could learn what their favorite, fashionable critics would have to say.

Sigi searched about him for some sign that would

reveal Moriarty's masked messenger, while Gambetti-Riccardo took his Jenny-Amelia by the hand.

The opera's hero sang:

"You got to first meet my mamma."

The heroine sang:

"I do?"

Sigi came to life when he suddenly spied a twisted lip on one of the singers in the chorus. Yes, it was Moriarty's messenger—it was Finney.

Gambetti sang:

"You got to sample her cooking."

Jenny sang:

"I'm not hungry."

The orchestra hit a particularly beautiful Verdi chord as Gambetti placed his hands under Jenny's armpits, partially supporting her breasts. He sang:

"Just try a little,
and *after*
—we'll hop into bed."

From among the make-believe crowd in the make-believe ballroom, a giant figure of a nobleman, dressed in black—the character called Renato (Amelia's lawful husband)—came up behind Gambetti, singing:

"You've got your hands
on my wife's BOOBIES!"

Gambetti reacted, vocalizing thusly:

"OY YOY!"

Renato drew his sword.

Jenny sang:

"RENA-TO!
I was just saying
so long to my cousin."

The chorus added:

> "Don't forget,
>   he is her cousin.
>   Sort of."

In Moriarty's box, Colonel von Stulberg tensely clutched his air gun. Onstage, Gambetti unclutched Jenny's boobies.

Jenny and the chorus sang:

> "RENA-TO!"

Renato, Gambetti, and Jenny faced each other, emotionally deep within their roles, as the chorus chanted:

> "Renato! Renato!
>   She don't fool around
>   —much!"

The henchman Finney, having heard his cue from the chorus, tilted his head and stood straight. He stepped forward, with mask, twisted lip and all, and opened his mouth to sing . . .

But Sigi, a far better musician, was well ahead of him on the cue and beat him to the lines:

> "WHY DON'T WE ALL DRINK
>   SOME VERY SEXY WINE?"

Finney, mouth still open, stared silently at the masked messenger opposite him, dumfounded.

For Orville, Sigi's singing also was a cue. With Holmes' first note, he opened a large pillbox and dropped pills into some wine goblets. So swiftly did the good man act, he was unobserved by the page who held the tray of goblets near Gambetti.

Gambetti drew the prop document with the blue ribbon from his belt, speaking his next line:

> "I GOT AN IDEA!"

Gambetti held up the prized document and sang:

"A new law—
Just be happy,
and no killing,
and be healthy—
And that's all!"

The costumed pages passed around the trays of wine goblets but, wildly contrary to Orville's expectations, *not* to the opera's characters nearest them. Instead, the four pages crisscrossed to new stage positions.

During that piece of choreography, the chorus sang:

"The Prince is one nice fellow.
The chicken was delicious.
Now we drink! Now we dance!
Let's hope we don't get sick!"

Everyone on stage drank. Orville Sacker became acutely upset when he saw Renato and some chorus singers across the stage from him getting the wine with the pills, while Gambetti, for whom the small white potions were intended, took a big swallow of undrugged wine.

The chorus hit three pleasing notes with:

"Salu-te!"

Gambetti was about to hand the document to Sigi. Before he could complete the gesture, however, Finney, who had remained in the background, stepped into a spotlight at a prominent point on the stage. Undaunted by his initial failure, or by his Irish accent, he sang:

"WHY DON'T WE ALL DRINK
SOME VERY SEXY WINE?"

Gambetti stopped himself in mid-motion, muttering a worried "Oh-oh!" to himself.

The same muffled, concerned sound dotted the auditorium: Moriarty muttered, "Oh-oh!"; the Russian muttered, "Oh-oh!"; and the Frenchman muttered, "Oh-oh!"

Now it was Sigi's and Orville's turn to be dumfounded. They stared at Finney.

Gambetti's eyes filled with suspicion. He held up the document again, speaking his first line, then singing, as before:

> "I GOT AN IDEA!
> A new law—
> Just be happy,
> and no killing,
> and be healthy—
> And that's all!"

The pages with trays again walked their choreographed crisscross patterns. Orville followed one of the pages until both were standing by Finney. He dropped a pill into the crook's goblet. A split second later, Finney looked at Orville, but the latter quickly pushed the pillbox against his nose and pretended he was taking snuff.

The chorus, well trained to never pass up a cue no matter what the circumstances, sang:

> "The Prince is one nice fellow.
> The chicken was delicious.
> Now we drink! Now we dance!
> Let's hope we don't get sick!
> Salu-te!"

The members of the chorus drank the wine. A skinny singer, who had sipped Orville's drugged wine, fell to one knee. At about the count of eight, he recovered and was able to stand again.

Gambetti was about to hand the *document* to Finney when Sigi stopped him short again, this time by singing in an Irish accent:

> "WHY DON'T WE ALL DRINK
> SOME VERY SEXY WINE?"

Gambetti was a picture of unblinking astonishment. There was an elongated silence, obviously never intended in the original Verdi score. The blackmailing musical connoisseur glanced toward the conductor, who shrugged his shoulders in despair.

In their box, the Russian and the Frenchman, smelling something rotten in Sweden, loaded an antique crossbow.

Gambetti, tired of staring at the conductor, tried staring at Finney, who kept his hand held out for the document. Then he had a go at staring at Sigi, who kept winking at him.

The Russian fired the crossbow.

Moriarty stood in his box and let out a loud, reverberating "YUH!" as an arrow whizzed into his box, landing between his legs.

The audience turned to look at the YUH! yelper, and his gunman, von Stulberg, quickly had to shove his air gun out of sight. The professor whispered into the colonel's ear and left the box.

On the great stage, the show's misused husband, Renato, having sipped a reckless amount of the drugged wine, keeled over.

The audience watched in rapt attention, sensing that they had spent their money on the most extraordinary interpretation of *A Masked Ball* any generation had ever seen.

Gambetti surveyed the fallen, prone Renato, then valiantly essayed his spoken line again:

"I GOT AN IDEA!"

He held up the document. The orchestra, with its conductor now sharing the general panic and confusion, was led into a faster tempo. Gambetti, accordingly, sang faster:

"A new law—
Just be happy,
and no killing,
and be healthy—
And THAT'S ALL!"

The pages broke into a trot to execute their crisscross, nearly busting into one another and dropping their trays. Orville dropped another pill into Finney's wine.

The exhausted chorus obligingly performed, leaving most of the talent it might once have had behind it:

> "The Prince is one nice fellow.
> The chicken was delicious.
> Now we drink! Now we dance!
> Let's hope we don't get sick!
> Salu-te!"

They drank. Three singers passed out. Then four more singers passed out.

Orville tried pushing Finney with one finger, naturally expecting him to keel over. But Finney just gave him a dirty look. Orville tried smiling back.

Finney, with the orchestra a few beats ahead of him, started to sing:

> "Why don't we all—"

Gambetti had had it, fed up even with his own artistic achievement. "SHUT YOUR MOUTH!" he yelled at Moriarty's man.

The weary pages mistook the leading man's shout for their cue and moved dizzily along their appointed paths.

The chorus was fatigued into a trance. But, upon seeing the pages move, it, in turn, concluded its bright moment had come again, and weakly sang:

> "The chicken is a fellow.
> The Prince was so delicious.
> Now we drink! Now we dance!
> Let's hope we don't get
> Sick!"

The dancers, not knowing up from down at that point, and nearly incapable of putting one foot before or after the other, carried Orville—under protest—offstage.

All but one of the singers dropped to the floor. The lone remaining singer, obviously a man of immense capacity for physical abuses, drank his wine and sang a historically brief solo:

> "SALU-TE!"

Gambetti raised his wine goblet.

Von Stulberg took aim at Gambetti.

The bullet from the nearly noiseless air gun pierced Gambetti's goblet.

Wine streamed from the goblet.

The impresario-singer now stood exactly in the middle between Sigi and Finney. He motioned them both to move a few inches away. He lifted a whistle hanging on a chain around his neck and stuck it in his mouth.

The conductor waved the orchestra on, stepping up the beat once more with his baton.

Gambetti threw the document in the air and blew his whistle: "Whee-ee-ee-eet!"

Sigi and Finney lunged into the air for the tossed document, just as latter-day competitors would jump for a basketball.

Gambetti bolted out of their way, behind Jenny.

The jumpers missed the document, which fell to the stage floor. They dove for it.

Gambetti, fearing for his life, grabbed Jenny around the waist. Jenny threw herself into her aria in an attempt, as was her habit, to overcome her own fear:

> "STOP THAT
> —you're such a tickle tease.
> You know
> —I'm superpassionate.
> Oh my, you make my heart go ZOW."

Miss Hill continued to wail Amelia's song as Sigi and Finney struggled for the document.

"Don't rip it!" Finney cautioned his opponent. "For Gawd's sake, don't rip it!"

> "Try to hold on to your sex urge."

Inspired by the proximity of Jenny's voice, Sigi

pulled Finney's chin into his knee. Finney collapsed, silently. Sigi found himself facing the audience, grasping the document in his hand.

The sharpshooting Colonel von Stulberg took careful aim, about to fire at Sigi. The youngest of the Holmes boys might have been the deadest but for the intercession of someone who proved again that blood is thicker than water.

A tall, slender man, smoking an enormous, drooping pipe, entered the box behind the lethal colonel. He placed a pistol behind von Stulberg's ear. The air-gun expert lowered his rifle, slowly turning to see his captor. His unholy eyes bulged in terror!

Chapter XVIII

CHAOS RULED. And not very well, as the opera came apart with a calamitous rush, piece by piece, note by note. The opera-house stage had been converted into an asylum.

Sigi, document in hand, was fighting to maintain a clear head in the midst of the danger and confusion. He tried to decide which way he might best make a quick exit from the stage.

Gambetti surrendered to hysteria.

Jenny helplessly looked at Sigi.

Sigi made for the stage-left wings, but stopped in the middle of his flight. For he spotted Moriarty, in mask and costume, coming at him menacingly from those very same wings.

The professor carried on his pitiless person a small pistol, which he carefully and cleverly concealed from the audience.

Sigi slowly backed up toward Gambetti and Jenny. Moriarty followed him steathily, pistol pointed, holding out his hand for the valuable document he had paid for.

Jenny and Gambetti felt their hearts jump and their terror triple when they spotted Moriarty's gun.

Suddenly, in an impromptu moment, Jenny grabbed Moriarty's outstretched hand, while Gambetti clung to her other arm for dear life. She led the hand with the pistol, and the two nefarious gentlemen, to the center of the stage. There she returned to Verdi's music and Gambetti's libretto, singing to her Riccardo:

"I WANT YOU NOW!
I WANT YOU NOW!
I WANT YOU NOW!"

Moriarty was temporarily stumped, too conscious of the audience to break from Jenny's grasp.

> "I WANT YOU NOW!
> FOR MY OWN
> —AND THEN—"

Gambetti, overtaken by the sincerity of her performance and guided by forces outside himself, belted out and joined in:

> "—AND THEN—
> OH BOY!"

Sigi backed off.

Moriarty caught sight of Sigi's retreat and watched him start to disappear off the stage, into the right wings—*with* the document. Audience or no audience, that was beyond the professor's patience.

BANG! A shot rang out.

Moriarty's gun smoked.

Sigi scurried. A bullet whizzed by him, missing his quick flesh only by inches.

Moriarty ran offstage in hot pursuit.

Gambetti fainted, clumping to the floor.

Jenny shook her singing partner and warbled:

> "Riccardo! RICCARDO!"

The conductor, all but out of his skull, turned the pages of the score in a frenzy, wondering if he had lost his place.

Jenny sang on:

> "Riccardo! RICCARDO!"

"Leave me alone," Gambetti pleaded with her under his breath.

BANG! Another shot rang out, this one from backstage.

The prone Gambetti opened one eye. "Shit!" he moaned.

Jenny, committed to finishing the final act, stretched out her aria and reached for her highest notes.

While *A Masked Ball* stumbled and fluttered on before its puzzled audience, Moriarty was conducting a backstage search. He gripped his gun, which was smoking again. He ran to a spiral staircase and rushed up the first few steps. He looked up, high up. Faintly, he could see and hear footsteps.

BANG! He had fired. And the fearsome sound careened around the metal staircase. He wound his way up the staircase, pistol steadily pointed.

When he was near the end of the staircase, the professor rushed to the top. There he found a door with a sign that read:

PROPS AND WARDROBE
STORAGE

He opened the door and cautiously entered.

The storage room actually was an attic at the top of the building. It had a slanted glass roof and the length of one wall was entirely windowed and open. Moonlight streamed in, creating weird shadows.

The attic housed masks, mannequins, suits of armor, prop tables, screens, costumes of all periods, character designs executed in water color, and an assortment of imaginative theatrical paraphernalia.

Moriarty closed the door behind him and slowly moved forward. It appeared as if every mannequin, every suit of armor, and all the faces of the paintings were looking directly at him.

He stopped when he spotted the shadow of two feet receding behind a screen.

BANG!
BANG!

The two shots from his pistol put two clean holes through the screen.

The professor waited a moment before proceeding to the screen. When he did venture to it, he knocked it over. Behind the screen was a stuffed dummy swinging from a chain. It wore a hat, belt, and sword on its otherwise unclothed body. Two holes pierced its painted heart, and blue tears seemed to fall from its painted face.

"WHOOOOO!"

Moriarty sprang around and fired.

BANG!

A ruffled owl flew out an open window.

The professor dashed to the window. "Bloody bugger bird bastard," he cursed. He watched the owl fly over the Thames below, and noticed the narrow ledges that ran along both sides of the window.

From somewhere in the attic, a voice spoke.

"A Webley's Number Two—"

The professor twisted around.

There was Sigi, mask removed, standing across from him. He was holding the document in one hand and his sword-cane in the other.

"—I think," Holmes continued, "carries only six cartridges."

Moriarity looked to his Webley's Number Two and fired. But the gun produced nothing more than a click.

"Yes!" said Sigi. "That's right. Six!"

"You're more shit smart than is healthy for you," the professor sneered. "I *used* to be the eleventh best fencer in Europe. Were ya aware of that?"

Young Holmes was not aware of that fact and registered some slight surprise.

Moriarty threw down his pistol and drew a sword from his opera costume. He swiped a single swipe at a nearby candle. Sigi lifted off the one-inch section his adversary had cut from the candle, then put it back on top of the candle.

"As you can see," Moriarty informed him, "this sword I'm carryin' is not a prop."

Sigi swiped two swipes at the candle. The professor lifted *three* small sections from atop the candle, and then replaced them.

"Neither is this sword," Sigi promised him.

His opponent swiped five quick swipes at the poor

candle, after which he gently toppled all of the candle sections over. Only a short stub remained.

"It sickens me ta shed useless blood," he said.

Sigi took five rapid swipes at the candle stub. The professor laughed, seeing that Sigi missed the stub entirely. But his mirth was cut short when Sigi demonstrated that he had *not* missed, by nudging the candle stub, causing five incredibly thin pieces to topple over.

"Buck up! Soon be over," Sigi announced.

"You're bein' used, ya know. Your brother meant ya only for a decoy."

"So it would seem."

"You will be careful with the document, won't ya, lad?" Moriarty asked his adversary, as they pointed swords at one another, ready to launch into fight. "It's no use to either of us if it gets damaged."

"I'll keep that in mind," Sherlock's brother answered politely.

Touché!?

Not quite.

For Finney stalked through the storage-room door. He pointed a pistol at Sigi.

"Drop your sword, Holmes!"

Sigi cursed.

Moriarty smiled.

"I said drop it, or I'll—"

Orville popped onto the scene, put a pistol to Finney's demented head, and finished his sentence for him: "—blow your brains out!"

Sigi smiled.

Moriarty frowned his blood-curdling frown.

Finney dropped his pistol.

Then Twisted Lip made a sudden turn and grabbed Sacker's hand. They struggled for control of Orville's pistol. Suddenly it went off!

PLOP!

A red flower popped out!

Both of the grapplers were startled.

Finney finally managed, "I always wanted one of

those." He then lunged for the real pistol, but Orville deftly kicked it backward, out of the room. The gun sailed down the spiral staircase.

Moriarty's sidekick, with professional smoothness, socked Orville three times smack in the face. "Ever box before, m'lad?"

Orville answered with, "A little." And delivered a combination—in the French style—of expert foot and fist blows.

The two prizefighters punched plain and punched fancy. Executing each blow with remarkable confidence and form, they furiously fought themselves right out of the storage room, leaving as abruptly as they had entered.

Chapter XIX

MORIARTY AND SIGI again had Timothy Hall's attic all to themselves.

One to one.

The challenge came.

"Well, let's try ya out, Mr. Holmes."

They fought mightily with their swords. It was true: both were expert swordsmen and fought extremely well. They thrust and parried around and around until they ended up on opposite sides of a large stored harp.

"Where did ya learn to fence? Ya have a peculiar style," Moriarty commented through the harp strings.

"Patricia Siddons Fencing Salon for Girls," Sigi answered. "I won the All-School Championship."

Their swords poked at each other through the harp, plucking out a few consecutive notes that sounded almost like a refrain from "The Blue Danube" waltz.

"Congratulations!" Moriarty saluted Sigi's musicianship.

"Thank you," Sigi saluted back.

They swung away from the harp and seriously had at each other again. The professor, during an awkward parry, accidentally stepped on a foot pedal, causing a connecting pair of cymbals to crash. A rusty CLANG! shook the attic windows.

A few moments later, Sigi lunged, piercing a large stuffed mannequin. Red sawdust poured from the dummy's belly.

Soon they locked swords. Moriarty shoved Holmes backward. Unfortunately, Sigi hit his head against a guillotine. The force of the blow almost knocked him out of his senses.

Moriarty gently placed Sigi's head, his brain numb,

on the guillotine's chopping block. "Lie down, son. Ya look a little tired."

Sigi tried to focus his bleary eyes, which he managed long enough to see a large, sharp-looking blade hovering above his neck. He turned over in semiconscious despair.

The professor stepped to the side of the death machine and sliced the taut rope that held the blade suspended. The guillotine blade swished down. But the Holmes head remained connected to the Holmes body, for the blade proved to be nothing but a gilded-rubber prop when it bounced several times off the back of Sigi's neck.

While his opponent cursed the blade, Holmes regained his strength and jumped up, ready to resume combat. He thrust and he lunged, forcing Moriarty up a short flight of prop stairs, at the top of which was a closed door marked EXPLOSIVES.

Using the door effectively, to lean against, Moriarty pounded his foot into Sigi's chest, sending him sprawling across the room. Hoping to find some new advantage, the evil mastermind quickly opened the door, turned into it, and found himself crashing into a brick wall. The impact shook the area.

From above the professor, a giant Mexican sombero dropped on his head. And below him, he discovered, stood a stuffed horse on wheels. He leaped from the prop stairs onto the stuffed horse's back, sending the wheels into forward motion.

From the other end of the storage room, Sigi could not believe what he saw coming toward him. It was an apparition of a wild Mexican on a steed, riding swiftly and brandishing a sword.

The ferocious horseman reached Sigi at full speed and took a great swing at his head. The alert detective adroitly ducked, avoiding what surely would have been one of the world's most severe headaches.

The Mexican horseman zoomed past Sigi, crashing into a painted backdrop, then falling against a wall lever. The impact on the lever forced it up, releasing a trigger.

Dozens of colored balloons fell from the ceiling, turning the drab storage room into a festival of color. The swordsmen slashed against the avalanche of balloons—Pop! Pop! Pop!—trying desperately to keep track of each other through the spray of rubber rainbow hues.

Meanwhile, along the catwalk high above the stage, the fighters' fighting seconds, Finney and Orville, were locked in their own fierce battle.

Finney forced Orville back. Then, Orville took the offense, forcing Finney back.

So they continued, alternating favored positions and upper hands. The scoundrel and the gentleman were a small study of the two contrary sides of man's nature, too evenly matched to forecast eventual triumph or defeat.

The balloon slayers finally reduced the fog of floating colored balls to the point where they could keep a fairly good account of each other's physical presence.

Moriarty backed Holmes to an open window, with the point of his sword much too close to the latter's throat for comfort. Sigi was forced to climb up and out of the storage room and onto the building's extremely narrow ledge. Moriarty followed.

The waters of the eternal Thames flowed majestically below.

"You're a little loose in the head, lad," the professor chortled. "It's not worth it."

He lunged. He plunged. His younger opponent parried. The action shot into high gear on the perilous ledge, neither combatant paying much attention to the sharp spikes sticking out from the side of the brick building.

Sigi, fate decreed, soon was forced to take account of the spikes, for after parrying beautifully to the left, right, and left again, he backed his right shoulder painfully into one of the steel protrusions.

Moriarty, keen scoundrel that he was, was swift to see his opening. He lunged, his whole body transformed into a straight dart. His sword penetrated Sigi's shoulder from the front.

Holed front and back, Sherlock's brother winced in pain.

"Careful of these spikes, son. They can hurt something awful," Moriarty mocked, withdrawing the point of his sword.

Through his pain, Sigi looked down, trying to calculate the drop to the river. It was a long-odds risk.

Moriarty paused to deliver a sermon. "It's very difficult to be a hero in real life. The villain usually doesn't behave the way he's supposed to."

Beads of perspiration formed on Sigi's forehead and above his upper lip.

The professor, confident now that the position as Europe's eleventh-best fencer was still his to claim, forced the fight on. But Sigi, his wound sapping his agility, could fight only defensively.

London's top villain lunged again, this time knocking the sword right out of his adversary's hand. Sorrowfully, Sigi's eyes followed his weapon's fall into the Thames.

"You were very good, son," the professor complimented him. "But you should always, *always* be thinkin' two and three moves ahead. Your brother's a master at it. Now, give me the document or I'll shove this sword right through your neck."

The bastard's reference to his brother's celebrated mind probably hurt Sigi more than the ripped flesh of his shoulder. But, at the moment, the psychology of the matter was far less important than Sigi's physical position.

Trapped on the tiny ledge, weaponless and hurting, he contemplated the Thames once more. The wind blew across his face. He handed Moriarty the prized document.

"I love pure reason," the victor sighed, smiling and taking the document from the vanquished.

The smirking smile was erased from Moriarty's face with dispatch. The obliterating force came when Sigi winked and pulled out another blue-ribboned, identical-looking document from inside his costume.

The professor scowled.

Sigi added further to the older man's confusion when he produced still another identical document. He now held one in his left hand and one in his right hand.

"Good, lad. Good! That's the idea," Moriarty congratulated him, obviously having regained his warped sense of humor. He then pulled out an identical document from inside his own costume. "I even had one myself. Just in case."

The good detective and the notorious criminal now each held two such documents.

"I wonder which is real?" the professor asked.

"Drop your sword or I'll throw mine into the river," Sigi threatened.

But Moriarty would brook no threat. He smiled his unique, crazy smile, raised the point of his sword so that it was aimed directly at Holmes' heart, and moved toward him.

Sigi, a man of his word, threw one of his documents into the river.

Moriarty promptly followed suit and threw one of his documents into the river.

Sigi was startled. What audacity, he thought to himself.

Moriarty was delighted.

"Just two left," he laughed. "This is fun."

Sword held straight, he moved closer to Sigi.

Sigi threw his second document into the river.

Moriarty threw his last document into the river.

"We both knew that there were four fakes on that prop table in the theater," the professor reasoned. "Now give me the real document that you took from Gambetti."

Sigi hesitated.

Moriarty put his sword point at the young man's shoulder and pushed.

"Give it to me, or I swear to Gawd I'll kill ya. An' I'm a good Catholic."

Sigi looked up to survey the giant, absolutely *mammoth* clock above them. It was, he could see, *one minute before eleven*.

With great hesitation, he reached behind his back and pulled out yet another blue-ribboned document from his belt. He handed it to Moriarty, wincing from the pain in his shoulder.

The triumphant criminal celebrated his supreme moment and kissed the document lovingly.

Sigi slowly clutched the spike that had wounded the back of his shoulder, as if the coldness of its hard steel helped to control his pain. He stole another glance at Saint Timothy Hall's huge clock above. The big hand of the clock was almost on 12.

Moriarty tauntingly raised the point of his sword until it rested once more on Sigi's throat.

"Good-bye, son," he said, smiling sweetly.

The big hand on the big clock jumped: it was exactly *eleven o'clock*.

!!!GONG!!!

The overwhelming sound of the clock crashed through the night air. A thousand and a thousand more vibrations sprang forth and the building's entire ledge shook.

!!!GONG!!!

Moriarty struggled to keep his balance on the trembling ledge.

!!!GONG!!!

While the professor's arms flailed wildly at the air, Sigi lifted a foot. With that foot, he gently pushed the sinister man off the ledge.

"Good-bye," said Sigi, politely.

Moriarty waved the document as he started to fall. "I STILL WIN, YA FOOL! . . ."

The body floated down through the vibrating air. It splashed into the storied Thames.

The big clock's ear-busting GONGs continued to ring out. They delivered both the correct time and the comforting message that virtue was at least alive, if not rewarded.

Chapter XX

SIGERSON WATCHED Professor Moriarty's not very graceful descent into the cold, rumbling river. Unable to determine whether the despicable old codger had swum or sunk, he climbed off the thin ledge and back into the theater's storage room.

A knock on the door greeted him.

"May I come in?" It was Orville, Sigi was relieved to hear.

"Certainly."

"How are you?" Sacker inquired, taking out a cigarette case.

"Never better. You?"

"Tip-top!" He was offering his friend a cigarette when he noticed the blotches of blood. "Sigi—you're hurt!"

"Just a scratch."

He lit Sigi's cigarette, then his own. "Any trouble with the big fellow?"

"Not much."

"Tell me, Sigi, where did you hide the real document?"

Sigi pointed. "In that suit of armor over there. Just lift the visor."

Orville strolled over to a nearby suit of armor. As instructed, he lifted the visor and pulled out the *real document!*

"It's a bloody good thing you thought ahead," said Orville.

They were startled by the next sound they heard.

"YUH! YUH!"

"The professor?" Sigi and Orville asked one another. They both looked toward the open window.

"YUH! YUH!" was heard again. The voice was distant, but it certainly was that of Moriarty.

Professor Moriarty was drenched like a mop, but alive. He stood on a barge some ways down the Thames, with a battered Finney by his side.

Moriarty was reading the fake document with which he had taken his long dive.

Not aware of what was false and what was real, Finney chose to congratulate his master. "You did it, boss. You outsmarted them all. You genius son of a gun."

Zwack! Baff! Plop!

A twitching Moriarty socked a startled Finney into the ageless river.

Sigi started for the door of the old prop room.

"Just put it on the table there, would you?" he asked Orville, indicating the valuable paper with the blue ribbon, the paper that might have plunged all of England into a catastrophe had he not rescued it.

"What do you mean?" Orville responded incredulously. "Aren't you going to give the document to Lord Redcliff?"

"I think," Sigi said, "it will be in his hands . . . in a few minutes."

"I don't understand," his companion responded, setting the document on a small, dusty table.

"Come along," Sigi invited him.

The two tired men left the dark room together. When their footsteps could no longer be heard, the silence was profound. The document rested on the table, the blue ribbon glimmering in the moonlight.

From a secluded corner, two shadows emerged— a tall, slender shadow and a stout shadow. The shadows revealed that two men were putting on their coats.

"Holmes!" Dr. Watson's voice demanded in the darkness. "Why didn't you do anything to help?"

"I would have—had the occasion arisen," the clipped voice of Sherlock Holmes assured the devoted chronicler of his achievements.

Chapter XXI

NATURE'S SWEETEST MOMENTS seemed to be on the brink of delivery on a particular day in one of London's fine parks.

The combination of sun-given energy and wisps of delicate air perked up even the most melancholy of dispositions. It was one of those days during which nothing should go wrong.

Sigi Holmes, seemingly as full of promise and energy as the day, was seen racing along a pathway, holding a telegram in his hand. He whizzed past strollers, nurses pushing baby carriages, and boys fishing, toward what must have been a very important goal.

Turning a shrub-decked corner, his destination was reached. Only a few precious feet down the path, Jenny sat, on the luckiest bench in the park. She looked petty enough to earn the envy of blossoms and birds.

Sigi ran directly up to and in front of the cherished lady. When he stopped, he was a little out of breath.

Jenny rose. The young man watched a dream stand and say, "Hello." He feasted his eyes upon the dream as it continued to speak. "What do you call this kind of a day? This is a crazy day!"

Sigi broke through his awe.

"Aren't you being married in a few minutes?" he asked.

"I most certainly am."

"Your cable said 'Urgent.'"

"'Urgent?' Is that what I said? I don't mean— I meant— What did I say? 'Urgent?'"

"Yes."

"I just wanted to say good-bye."

"Good-bye," he said, trying his hardest not to sound crushed.

"Good-bye," she said.

Jenny walked off, around the bend; a beautiful genie disappeared in the crisp air.

Sigi melted onto the bench. He sat contemplating—with a fervor he had never experienced before. Silence carressed him, soon followed by the park's lively noises of animals and the distant, playful voices of boys.

A stout old man, who was pushing a harp on casters, appeared from around the curve. He was followed by a tall old man, who was carrying a violin.

The time-worn pair of musicians chose to stop at Sigi's bench. However, instead of disturbing his reverie, they somehow seemed to contribute to it.

The tall one of the duo took off his hat and set it down, face up on the ground, for donations. The old violinist and the old harpist played. Their selection just happened to be a favorite of their audience of one. It was the old music-hall hit, "But You Can't Love As I Do."

Sigi stared at the old man playing the violin. The old man playing the violin stared back at Sigi. With his large, narrow foot, he nudged his hat toward the blue-eyed, blond-haired bachelor.

Sigi, still in a semihypnotic state, stood up and reached into his pocket. He looked at the little bit of change he had, and tossed it for a while in his hand, before dropping it into the old man's hat.

The musicians continued their song while their sole listener walked away. But, halfway to the curve in the lane, the young man was stopped by the reappearance of the dream: Jenny was just rounding the same curve and coming toward him.

"Now," Jenny entreated, confused, "what the hell am I supposed to do?"

Sigi smiled. "Would you care to dance?"

And—with the generous assistance of the harp, the

violin, the park sounds, the breeze, and the light of the sun—dance they did.

The old violinist took off a false eyebrow and scratched the real brow behind it as he watched his brother dance.

Orville Sacker, another of the universe's best souls, strode around the curve in the park path. He walked up to Sherlock. They looked into each other's eyes, steadily, as only principled men who have done their best can.

Sherlock nodded a quiet thank-you, then traded a glance with Dr. Watson, the harpist, without either of them missing a note of their music.

Inspired, perhaps by the elegance of the day, their song soared.

Sigi and Jenny soared, too, dancing and kissing beneath a picture-book sky.

Jenny was breathtaking in giving the gift of her love. And Sigi—bless him—*was,* after all, among the smartest of men, for he knew now how to love in return.

THE PLAYERS

Sigi...........................Gene Wilder
Jenny.....................Madeline Kahn
Orville Sacker.............Marty Feldman
Gambetti ....Dom DeLuise
Moriarty.....................Leo McKern
Finney.......................Roy Kinnear
Lord Redcliff.............John Le Mesurier
Sherlock Holmes...........Douglas Wilmer
Dr. Watson................Thorley Walters

Produced by
Richard A. Roth

Directed by
Gene Wilder